TRIALS
TO
TRIUMPH

God Always Has A Plan

OSIANDER ROSE

Printed in the United States of America.

Library of Congress Control Number: 2022935060

ISBN	Paperback	978-1-68536-449-6
	Hardback	978-1-68536-450-2
	eBook	978-1-68536-711-4

Westwood Books Publishing LLC
Atlanta Financial Center
3343 Peachtree Rd NE Ste 145-725
Atlanta, GA 30326

www.westwoodbookspublishing.com

For my family,
Thanks for always supporting me
Thanks for always trusting in God

Other Books by Osiander Rose

A World of Words Works
Preaching to the Tenth Pew Parts 1, 2, 3, and 4
God, Where Are My Muscles?
The Usual Crowd
A Boat in the Desert
Choose Your Weapon, Choose Your Side

TABLE OF CONTENTS

PROLOGUE

The sun wasn't shining as bright today. The rain poured heavily but, Standford Mon didn't feel the drench through her baby-blue pants and her favorite lilac and cream-colored blouse. Her muscular forty-eight-year-old body shivered, not from the cold but from the parole board's decision to let her only child finally go free ahead of his seven-year sentence. She wiped the expensive massacre from her smooth skin. She didn't even need to wear makeup to look fabulous. Yet, each day she caked the mud and liquids on her already beautiful face, stepping out of the house looking like the next top model ready for the cover of a popular magazine.

The rain slowed. The sun strained unsuccessfully to put rays of warmth on its passersby. Today was another one of the terrible days in her life. It was as though she'd completed it before it really began. Prayer had not come easy, but it did come. She tried to remember if she thanked God or simply scolded Him for not allowing victory to come sooner and as promised. Yes, she understood it to be promised and waited patiently each day for it to come. Perhaps she was running out of patience, which is never a good sign when one is trusting in the Lord. Trying not to remember how long she'd been waiting, she let the time come to the front of her mind; it had been several years. To be exact, it would soon be *seven* years. But who was counting? Surely not Abraham. She'd learned about the patience of Abraham several years ago while at Bible study. She'd been forced to attend with her parents. She couldn't have been older than fifteen. It had been the same night she planned to skip athletic study hall to hang out with her potential boyfriend. She hadn't even mentioned it nor shown any signs of the rendezvous. Yet, somehow, Devesta Morris knew it in her heart and Mr. Derrick Morris went on and said it out loud.

"Standford, you need to come with me tonight. Whatever you planned for this evening can wait. They'll find out at school tomorrow that you couldn't make it." Standford said nothing, so Derrick continued, almost laughing. "Are you going to eat what your mother made for dinner?"

Standford stood there, hoping her mouth wasn't wide open with shock.

At last, she managed a neutral-sounding, "Yes, sir." She laughed a little about the dinner remark and watched her very handsome father head for the kitchen making no eye contact. Derrick Morris wore a pair of work jeans and a dress shirt. He was the kind of man who made everything look good even if it was dirty, which happened to be the present case. Standford laughed to herself as she thought back on all the times her classmates or friends were like, "Ooh, is that you dad? My gosh, he's handsome." Her father remained humble and just smiled, greeted them politely, and walked away. He did just that this afternoon; he smiled at her and walked away. Standford wanted to make sure he wore fresh clothes. She hoped he'd change for Bible study.

It had to be Wednesday. Derrick Morris met up with Devesta Morris in the kitchen to get ready for dinner. Standford stood in the doorway of the living room for a few more moments, trying to understand what had just happened.

Derrick Morris smiled at her from the kitchen and continued with the quick dinner. She returned the sincere smile and headed downstairs to study and get some homework done before leaving with her parents for Bible school. Standford Morris (Mon) was a smart student, making good grades and demonstrating good behavior, but she would soon abandon her studies for what she considered the better things in life. Nonetheless, she knew she'd better go to Bible study as requested, especially if her dad made mention of it specifically like he had today. Standford knew well that Derrick Morris didn't make unnecessary comments. He meant precisely what he said.

She finished most of her studies, changed, ate the quick dinner, and was ready to go when her dad called out her name on his way to the car.

That night, long ago, the Bible school teacher stood before the small group of dedicated members telling the story of Abram. "It had been twenty-four years before the promised miracle of God came to Abram."

Standford thought, *How could I let Satan win again? Would that set me back to the beginning?* God couldn't be that cruel, and she didn't want to not win regardless of how long it took. If Abram waited on God for twenty-four years, then surely, she could wait for another one. "But I'm not Abraham. I don't have Abraham's patience," she said into the air. "Have I even done what needs to be done to have God grant me such a miracle?" A tear began to form on her left cheek, ready to mix with the rain and her smeared makeup. Somehow, she had to stay in the fight and not give up on God's promises. She suddenly realized how much she missed her father. Mr. Derrick Morris was a great man of God. He was also such a happy and handsome man. He would know what to tell her. Sadly, he was no longer around to rescue her from the problems she felt she was unable to solve. The tears formed more rapidly. One because she missed her dad and two because she lost her son for about seven years.

"Miracles happen every day, Standford." She could hear his voice in her mind's eye. "You must be in a position to receive them. And you really have to be patient." That was her biggest issue: patience.

She wiped her face of rain and tears and looked toward Heaven. "These rocks will soon be rubies," she shouted into the skies. She intended for the Devil and all his human followers to hear her. "These rocks will soon be rubies," she shouted again but louder. A young lady made eye contact and frowned incessantly, making sure she knew that it wasn't okay to pray out loud and especially while in public. Standford smiled back suddenly feeling dry. The rain continued to pour as she made her way to the courthouse. She wanted to smile, thinking of her dad and how he would feel about her trusting in God but decided against it, for this wasn't the time to think about him. She had to think about her only son. The trip up the stairs seemed an eternity. She felt like she was moving in slow motion, though everything and everyone around her was moving at a much faster pace.

Today just might be the day. She told herself to be prepared to accept whatever God gave them. The young lady's frown seemed to finally fade. She yelled out once more about the rocks and rubies, took in the stares and growls of annoyance, and placed her hand on the brass handle of the St. Paul City Prison administration building. She made her way to the ladies' room to fix her face back to its top-model original and looked for her husband, Ninx Mon. "Maybe, maybe not, and if not, I have to keep trusting," she whispered. As she slowly wiped her face clean, she took a moment to remember how it all began.

CHAPTER 1

In the Beginning

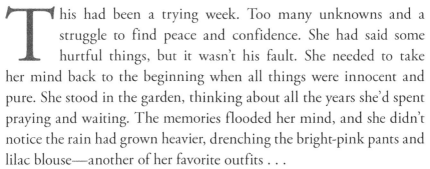

T his had been a trying week. Too many unknowns and a struggle to find peace and confidence. She had said some hurtful things, but it wasn't his fault. She needed to take her mind back to the beginning when all things were innocent and pure. She stood in the garden, thinking about all the years she'd spent praying and waiting. The memories flooded her mind, and she didn't notice the rain had grown heavier, drenching the bright-pink pants and lilac blouse—another of her favorite outfits . . .

When she realized that she'd walked to the greenhouse and back, she headed into the house to shower and change. Standford sat close to the big favorite window. She wasn't sure whether it was a day to celebrate, break down in tears, or ask God again, "Why?" The long navy-blue sundress clung to her lightly-muscled body, which was ten pounds less than she'd been carrying last month. She hadn't taken up a specific diet. The stress and worry took away the weight. That wasn't healthy weight loss, and Standford of all people knew it.

NaCharles' hearing was in four hours. Squinting at the midday sun, Standford hand-pressed the strategically placed flowers on the dress. It was a hard rain for the middle of June.

This is my favorite window. I can stand and talk to the Lord and sit and wait for my answer. She quickly wiped an unexpected tear as she thought about NaCharles' fate. *Lord, what will the judges tell me today? Then, what do I do with their response?*

The steaming sound of the coffeepot interrupted her next thought. "I'll be right back so we can continue," she said as she looked up at the ceiling of her home. Two years ago, she and Ninx Mon had separated, claiming irreconcilable differences. At least that's what they told the judge. A year later, they divorced after being married for sixteen wonderful years. She wanted to think about what got them to where they were now, but it was too painful. It would have been easy to understand and recover if it had been infidelity, unemployment, chronic illness, or the usual lost love. Yet, it was none of those. Ninx was a good husband and an excellent father. She stuck with the story of irreconcilable differences—vague and safe. Their only son, NaCharles Mon, was fifteen. He took it very hard and started to do some wild things. Nothing major. Just enough to get their attention and just enough attention that they had to come together to resolve it. Each time they did and did so congenially.

She had promised herself that she wouldn't think about how she got to today, she allowed her mind to go back again to see where she could've made a difference. As the cup of coffee cooled on the counter, she cautiously let her mind drift, even though it was painful.

On that dreadful day, it had been too early in the morning for anyone's phone to ring unless there was danger. Standford remembered sitting up in her king-sized bed. As usual, the pillows were bunched in the left corner, and the covers lay stacked at the foot with the satin bonnet daggling on her left foot. She would have laughed to herself, but the ringing of the cell phone was a nervous distraction. She'd scrambled to pick it up, cutting off Isaac's "But God" ringtone and half-hoping it wasn't Ninx telling her they had another NaCh issue. That had gone on far too long, and he rarely called or came by to see her. Terribly worried but trying not to sound breathless, she said hello as if it were 1:00 in the afternoon and not the very early hours of the morning.

"Hello," a strange voice replied. "Is this Standford Mon?" When she said nothing, the voice continued, "The parent or guardian of NaCharles Mon?" The voice on the other end sounded surprised that she didn't start cursing him for calling in the middle of the night—no doubt he'd been called a few choice names and told a few choice things over the years.

Standford glanced at the bedside clock, which read 1:30 a.m. Not a good sign on a Tuesday but not too terrible, given that NaCharles was twenty-three years old now, living on his own, and supposedly had a pretty decent job. "Yes, why?" she finally said. She surprised herself with how calm she was, given the hour. She hoped she didn't come off as snappy—she didn't know who was on the other end. "I'm sorry, but who are you, and how'd you get this number?" she added, trying to be polite.

"My apologies, ma'am." She thought she heard a smile in his voice. "I'm Detective Richard Larry Wingsong from the Garden City Police Department." Standford wondered why he said his full name. So awkward. She let him continue. "We have reason to believe that your son, NaCharles Mon, was involved in a bank robbery last night, leaving a victim fighting for his life."

Detective Richard Larry Wingsong paused to allow Standford to digest the information.

What had he just told her? She couldn't bring herself to speak just yet. Her breathing had become heavy and choppy. She looked again at the bedside clock, which now read 1:32 a.m. Only two minutes had passed, but it seemed like hours. She felt herself staring down at the print of her cotton pajamas. She could hear herself laugh about them— they were a present from her ex-husband and their son. She tried to forget that Detective Richard Larry Wingsong held the receiver on the other end, expecting her to respond. She looked at her bedside clock and couldn't believe she was having a conversation with a detective so early in the morning, so early in the week. She needed to pull herself together long enough to respond to the detective, but first, she needed to take a moment. She took that moment to think a back on a time she didn't make a good decision . . .

How had Derrick Morris known that she was going to leave the house with her well-planned lie and meet up with DM near the library? She would tell her parents that she was going to athletic study hall at the library, which would be true in a sense. She then planned to meet DM outside and ask him to go steady with her. All the other girls had a boyfriend; why couldn't she? It was taking too long. and she'd decided to speed up the process. Mr. Morris didn't insist that she go with her parents that night. Instead, he'd asked out of courtesy with a hint of command. Standford knew he asked for a reason beyond what she understood. In the end, it was a good thing he asked at all.

Standford finally spoke, but it sounded more like a question than a response. "Yes, Detective Richard Larry Wingsong, I hear you but, what do you need of me?" Another unbearable pause. Standford took the silence to brace herself for the worst: robbery victim fighting for his life. Last night. When? Where? Why?

"To be honest, Mrs. Mon, I'm not sure yet." Standford noticed the change in his voice. She was about to correct the *Mrs.* to *Miss* but decided against it. This wasn't the time for proper salutations. For the most part, she felt relieved; perhaps it wasn't that bad.

"We're still waiting for more details. An eyewitness gave one of my officers NaCharles' name and a rough description—your son being one of the two men. I just don't want you to be blindsided when the details become public and your son is named the possible male perpetrator."

"Thank you, Detective," Standford stammered, hoping she didn't sound too relieved and wanting so badly to add, "Let's hope it's not him." A twosome. That made things even worse. He had probably partnered up with the wrong people . . . or person. A twosome. The details weren't available. No additional details had come out yet. To recover, she asked, "So, what do you want me to do now?"

"Good question. We'll have a team locate NaCharles. Our hope is that he's willing to cooperate. I hope we can have you and Mr. Mon's full cooperation, Mrs. Mon."

Standford felt devastated. "Cooperate" meant that he most likely had a part in this alleged crime.

"Mrs. Mon, if he contacts you in any way, please encourage him to contact the station. Like I said, we don't have specific details—just his name and a sketchy description as one of the robbers. But he can clear his name if it isn't him. Also, before you say it, you'll be the first to know if *we* come to know more than I've already shared."

Standford stumbled to sound confident that it wasn't NaCharles, but there was depressed hope in her voice. When the line went silent, Standford glanced at the bedside clock. It was only 1:37 a.m. The conversation seemed to have lasted an eternity nonetheless. The moment she pressed the end call button, her head began to swim wildly. She thought of all the times her dad had told her, warned her, protected her, from doing evil and from evildoers. Her head began to ache. At age forty-five, she still longed for a word from her dad when she was in these kinds of situations.

The early morning minutes passed by slowly. She gathered up her pillows, placed her silk bonnet back on her escaped hair, and reached for her blanket, which felt heavier than it needed to be. She almost cried but decided against it. She wanted to call Ninx, but now wasn't a good time. She lay restless on the bed, thinking about a hot Sunday afternoon.

"Don't fret because of evildoers. Although they do evil, God laughs at them. They aren't going to get away."

The small church was way too warm for a Sunday in July. There were two windows on either side of the church fellowship space straining to provide some comfort to the twenty-some members gathered. Devesta wore a baby-blue two-piece outfit with an ankle-length skirt and a baby-blue and gold hat that looked like a hornets' nest. It was way too big for her to sit in the front blocking the view of the six children that sat behind her. Derrick Morris wore a plain black three-piece suit with a gold handkerchief hanging lifelessly from his right breast pocket. His big hat was placed on the coat rack when they entered. He told his son to make sure no one took it. They sat close to each other as if still in love from the very first time they met. The siblings laughed in jest, but Standford smiled with joy. They looked marvelous together.

The preacher's voice boomed across the pews of the small church. Standford looked up to see a five-foot-four dark-skinned preacher in

5

the pulpit. He opened his dark-blue suit jacket to expose a lilac dress shirt with big sweat stains in the arm pits. He handed the suit jacket to the minister on his left and then wiped his face with what looked like a lilac handkerchief. He adjusted his dark-blue matching pants that were too long for his stature and stepped up to the microphone on tiptoes. The minister to his right quickly adjusted the microphone so that the preacher of the hour could stand flat and speak. His voice was a lot heavier than his small stature.

"Don't fret, saints. God will not let evil befall you and let the Devil escape with your joy." The preacher looked about the congregation, who for the most part appeared shocked at the sound of his magnified voice in comparison to his barely five-foot height, as if he'd begun a sermon not meant for today or not meant for the members present. The extended pause was awkward; the congregation was patient.

He finally let go of the silence. "First, John 2:15-17 talks about the pattern of the world. We simply need to read the word, sing God's praises, pray to God the Father, and live the Word. Saints, if we don't love the things that are in the world, we don't have to fret because of evildoers." The preacher paused and looked about the congregation. He almost took to his toes again but decided to step to the right side of the pulpit so that all could see him.

There's no need to fret if you're not of the world. The connection was perhaps obvious to most of the congregation. Standford struggled to understand the preacher's meaning and intended direction. She tried not to place too much attention on his height, which appeared to distract a majority of the congregation, and when he spoke, that made paying attention that much harder to maintain. She closed her eyes to concentrate on what he said versus the fact that he could barely see over the pulpit.

"Saints, if you love the world more than God, then God is not in you—hence the lack of fear—and the excitement of doing evil consumes you." The preacher read the rest of verse seventeen; He who does the will of God stays with him forever.

Standford tried to take in the consequences of doing evil. She just didn't know if NaCharles was the evildoer or if he was amongst evildoers watching them do the evil deed. In the end, none of the evil was good, and none of it would result in a happy ending. She returned her thoughts to the moment.

Was it too early to call NaCharles? She looked at the ruffled covers as if to get an answer from them. She decided to wait for a *better* time in the morning to call. What *was* a better time? Detective Wingsong had no problem with 1:30 a.m. Sighing, she dialed the number. The voice message sang out, *"This is NaCharles. Do nothing. I'll hit you back."* The beep came too quick. Standford lost her words. "Call me, please," she stammered into the phone, unsure if her voice sounded calm. She hoped he'd sense an emergency when he got around to listening to the message. He would probably come by the house as opposed to calling her back. Standford fought sleep, knowing that she needed sufficient rest for what was perhaps to come later on in the morning.

It had been quite some time, it seemed, since NaCharles' name was associated with the police department. It truly had been a long time. She always assumed no contact was a good day for the Mons. She had been getting used to not hearing from him, which caused her to worry less. She knew NaCharles wasn't a model citizen. He started getting into trouble at school more when he was around twelve and with the law when he was sixteen. She and Ninx still attributed his not-so-good choices to their divorce. That excuse was perhaps a bit off but convenient enough to help them cope. NaCharles nearly dropped out of school at one point. He was just in sixth grade. The school called her and her husband constantly. They were contacted by the teachers, the in-school suspension supervisor, the dean of students, the associate principal, and the principal. They even got a few calls from the police officer assigned to the school. *How could a handsome and smart twelve-year-old get into this much trouble almost daily?* Standford thought to herself. She tried to smile in her sporadic sleep as she thought about her son and their plight to get him to age twenty-three alive—well . . . and *not* in trouble with the law. As a bonus out of serious trouble.

She thought about all the times she vowed not to compare his rearing to hers. She vowed that she would do her own parenting. *Good* parenting. Devesta and Derrick did what they thought was best for her. She still managed to mess that up for them, and now her son was probably doing the same to her. Sitting in bed fully awake now made her think that it wouldn't have been a bad idea to treat her child like Derrick Morris did her; maybe partially. He knew what to say and when to say it. He wasn't judgmental and with guidance and teaching, left all the final decision-making up to her. She never felt as if he was trying to get her to be like him or conform totally to his idea of childrearing. As she looked into the dark of her bedroom, she wondered what process of childrearing could have made all the difference? Derrick Morris didn't pass judgment on her as a child or as an adult. In her thoughts, she then changed her mind. She was right to do her own parenting, and she was almost certain Derrick Morris would tell her the same if he were still alive. She took a moment to think back when . . .

Devesta gracefully walked by Standford and whispered, "Your Dad knows best. Be sure to bring your Bible and your school books with you if you haven't completed all of your homework. Are you walking or riding with us? He told you to come with us tonight for a reason. Not sure yet why, but you'll know soon enough." Standford returned a warm smile. She wasn't upset and complied without question. Yes, her mother was right. He told her that for a reason. *She'd* soon know why. Maybe tonight or later. She knew it would come.

In the darkness, she thought about NaCharles in grade school, where he'd been suspended more times than his age by December of his sixth-grade year. It was unbelievably awful.

"Hello, Mr. and Mrs. Mon. Yes, it's NaCharles again. Such a handsome young man."

Standford would look into her husband's eyes and cry in her heart. Mrs. Peddleton would always begin the conversation with something positive. It was genuine, and her voice was soft. They all knew that NaCharles had done something drastic for which he would get suspended. All they were there to do was get the paperwork and see how many days—two, five, seven? They'd heard each of those numbers more than once throughout the school year.

It was November. This would be NaCharles' twelfth suspension for the school year. Mrs. Peddleton moved about her manicured office, shuffling papers as if the papers for the Mons had been misplaced. She was always well-dressed. Nothing like an elementary school principal but more like an affluent politician always on the campaign trail. Her nails were golden rust today and of reasonable length. She wore a satin rust-colored scarf and an expensive-looking beige two-piece skirt and vest. The buttons reflected from the weak sunlight coming through the office window. Her dark-blue blouse with quarter-length sleeves had ruffles peeking from her vest. She smelled like a perfume store with distinctively separate scents. Standford could clearly smell Stunned and Beautiful; she too owned a bottle of each fragrance. *How can I do that?* thought Standford as she watched her rearrange another stack of papers. Her glowing skin and dancing movement showed no signs of disgust that NaCharles would receive another suspension.

"Aw here it is," she finally belted out. She looked at Ninx and Standford, who then touched hands. They were both thinking the same thing (stalling for time due to embarrassment).

"Don't be embarrassed on our account Mrs. Peddleton. We know that Ridgeview and your staff are doing all they can to support our son. We're doing all we can as well to include praying to God for a miracle in his life." Standford didn't care about mixing church with state. She needed to let Mrs. Pendleton know that NaCharles' behaviors were of his own doing and that prayer was their primary course of action. Mrs. Peddleton held the suspension paperwork and forced a smile at the parents.

"Yes, I know, Mr. and Mrs. Mon. I have no doubt that you're doing all you can, and you also know that I cannot respond to how you're getting things done." She winked at Ninx.

This was not the day to tell Ninx that Mrs. Peddleton probably had a secret crush on him. He no doubt was a handsome man. Many women ogled him, and some even made comments about whether he was alone or with Standford. His crazy green eyes and smooth light skin caused eyes to raise or heads to turn. Today, Ninx wore a light green 511 shirt and khaki pants. His chiseled chest pressed against the material of the shirt and his fully formed thighs straightened out the faint wrinkles in his khakis. Standford had done her own secret double-take on their way out of the house. "I can look all I want too," she reminded herself.

The Mons left Ridgeview with NaCharles in tow. No one spoke as they drove home. The thirty-minute ride seemed longer going back. After about the sixth suspension, Ninx told everyone that there would be no more screaming and blaming. Everyone would give the situation twenty-four hours and then a small family meeting would be held at a neutral location. Ninx selected the locations. He said that the Mon home was a safe haven and wouldn't be filled with negative energy. They would say a prayer on the way out and then drive to the selected location and have the meeting. By April of the following year, Mon had literally run out of locations to hold the family meeting.

Standford cried in her sleep. She thought back on how she and Ninx held onto their small amount of faith and prayed for their son to "get better," "do better," and "be better". Had God forsaken them, or did they just need to be patient? NaCharles didn't seem bothered by the amount of stress the situation was causing. How could he? He was only twelve years old.

The dampness on her face awakened her. She glanced at her cell phone, which was miraculously still in her hand. Her hair bonnet was on the pillow next to her. She briefly laughed at the bonnet when she noticed she'd only been asleep for forty-five minutes.

She decided she'd call NaCharles in another hour. If he still had his job, then she could catch him before he went to work. She tried to remember the last time they spoke since he started dating Masha. It would be awkward but necessary she told herself. There was also the possibility he'd heard her message and would come over. She didn't think their relationship was severed to the point that he wouldn't come if she'd called him. The relationship was not on the best of terms and perhaps on the way to being badly damaged since he met Masha. For Standford, sleep hadn't come. At eight o'clock in the morning, she was sitting straight up in bed. Moments later, she searched frantically for her cell phone to check for messages. None.

"Who's going to find out NaCh? This will be the last run, and then we can move on to bigger and better things."

"Like what? You told me the last time that this is the last run and we can move on to bigger and better things and we're still here." NaCharles looked into the eyes of the thirty-two-year-old Masha. Masha, twelve years older, had told NaCharles that she was eighteen when she was really twenty-eight years old at the time. Standford knew that something wasn't quite right when she first met Masha at the pawn store across town but, every time she tried to tell NaCharles, he resisted and didn't want to hear anything negative about Masha; especially from his mother. They started spending a lot of time together after Standford and Ninx's divorce. She was afraid to tell Ninx. He eventually found out too late. NaCharles, by then, was head over heels for Masha. Standford felt in her spirit that Masha wasn't telling the truth about her age and a few other things. NaCharles barely graduated from high school as promised and refused to attend even a community college. If he was trying to hurt her because she and Ninx were not together, it definitely wasn't working.

It was two years into the scams when NaCharles found out Masha's real age. He'd been tasked with bringing the getaway car to the crime scene. Masha had left her purse in the car this particular time when she usually carried everything in her pocket or a small pocketbook. NaCharles was overwhelmed with curiosity that stemmed from his mother getting on him about everything wrong with Masha, including her real age. He read her Minnesota driver's license and found out two things; she wasn't twenty years old, and she wasn't from California. He was devastated and relieved at the same time. By then, he was so crazy about her, he was neither angry nor surprised. He never spoke a word to her or his mother about where she was from or her true age.

When the run was complete, Masha jumped into the getaway car, kissed him on the cheek and they drove to the rally point. NaCharles appeared as eager and energized as usual. Masha asked no questions, and he made no comments. All the times before, he was never bothered by either her age or what she did for a living. Somehow today was different. For some strange reason, he couldn't fathom why it was such a bother. They were supposedly in love—ride or die dogs. He suddenly missed his mother and his father.

He replayed the argument as he watched Masha eagerly prepare for her so-called "last run."

"Mom, you don't understand. I really love this girl!"

"*Woman*," Standford corrected quickly. "She is a *woman*, NaCharles. That girl as you call her is a woman. I may not be able to prove it now, but I will in due time. She is *not* eighteen." Standford knew she had pushed too far too hard too fast. In the end, she knew he would do something bad to spite her. She wished he wouldn't but knew he would.

"You just don't want to see me happy and in love," NaCharles shouted across the sitting room. "You just don't like that she's prettier than you and that she understands me much better than you!" They stood, looking at each other for a moment. NaCharles added, "And she's young." He tried to hold back the tears. Crying wasn't manly—especially not in the presence of his mother and on the subject of a girl. NaCharles meant for his words to sting. He was so angry with her and his Dad for trying to take away the one thing he had good going for himself: family. Standford, on the other hand, wasn't bothered by any of the statements except, "And she's young." Standford decided against speaking her next thought. She let it go. Standford knew that today wasn't the time, and the moment wouldn't yield the results she wanted. Instead, they both stood in the middle of the sitting room, steaming with emotions. In the end, NaCharles did go with the girl that Standford knew in her heart was already a woman.

The argument between NaCharles and Standford matched the one earlier between her and Ninx. Standford stood eloquently in the middle of the room as the sun slowly faded in the background. She was beautiful even in frustration. She cared for both Ninx and

NaCharles. The baby-blue blouse and faded jeans intended for a peaceful conversation didn't result in as much. Ninx and Standford yelled at each other about time, jobs schedules, careers, and NaCharles.

Now she and NaCharles continued the conversation.

"Well mom, me and that woman will be together. She loves me like you loved Dad. Why can't you just be happy for me? I'm twenty years old. I can handle myself." NaCharles paused to look in the direction of Standford. He knew he had a beautiful mother inside and out. He also knew that his father was stubborn as most men he knew. He didn't want to tell his mother that he knew that Masha was much older than she told him but he loved her anyway. He continued while the thoughts flowed. He decided that today wasn't the time, and his real thoughts wouldn't yield the intended results. He continued on a different thought path.

"I know you don't think she's right for me, but I think she's right for me." Standford was sure not to cry in front of her son. She was still angry and frustrated and she felt that Masha was hiding something and being outright deceitful to her son. She considered the conversation she had with her parents when she first met Ninx. She too had been warned by Ninx's mother to stay away, but she stayed with him in spite of how both parents felt. Now, here she stood in a *déjà vu* situation with her own son. She didn't think she could take another generation of failure. Masha appeared and carried herself far too maturely for the age she claimed to be when Standford first met her. At that time, Standford just couldn't place her finger on it, and today in the front room, she still didn't have it exactly but she still knew it was something.

"NaCh, something's just not right about Masha. Of course, she's gorgeous, clever, and evidently loves you as you claim but, something doesn't add up here. She didn't finish high school. She has no job but buys you things. Where are her parents? And why haven't we even met them yet? You haven't even met them." Standford closed the space between her and NaCharles. The tears had dried and taken up residence at the bottom of her cheeks. "I'm just not comfortable, I worry about you, and I don't think you're ready."

NaCharles faced the living room window, still listening to his mother. He knew she was right. It took him a couple of years, but he knew in his heart that she was right about most of the things she'd said. He wasn't however, ready to tell her so—not now. He would, he promised to himself, soon. This just wasn't a good time.

Masha had dressed and quickly ran through the details of the so-called last job. NaCharles still loved her as he had years ago. Standing at the window today was a twenty-year-old boy struggling emotionally to find his place in the world. He briefly thought of his parents when they were together and happy. He thought about all the arguments he had with his mother about Masha—about his decision-making. They'd both said hurtful things to each other. He even let his mind go to the time his parents' divorce was official. He remembered how everything had changed. He'd met Masha or Masha had chosen him. He tried to recall. Perhaps their relationship had been the result of the divorce and his feelings about it. Today, he wasn't sure.

Now it was hard to say anything. He couldn't help the feelings he had for her, yet he had an odd feeling that something wasn't quite right. He felt that emotional tugging feeling he had when he and his mother had argued about what Masha was not. He refused to acknowledge that his mother was right about most of it and that he was in denial about all of it.

Minutes passed. In the midst of his thoughts, Masha came in to join him at the kitchen window. She smelled of pure beauty and innocence. He turned to her to see that her physical appearance matched her smell. She only hugged him this time, whispering in his ear, "Promise, Toots. This is the last run." NaCharles put up his defenses, hoping it didn't show on the outside. No kiss and rubs this time? Strange already. No ruffling of the hair and telling him "You're a minor, there's nothing they can do to you?" Even stranger.

"Is it?" NaCharles wasn't so sure. That odd feeling still nagged at him. He knew he loved her with all his heart, but something still told him that there was or would be a problem with this "last run." He smiled lovingly at her and returned to his thoughts, staring out of the

kitchen window. She seemed to silently understand his uneasiness with this last run. She touched him lightly on his still shoulder and headed out of the kitchen, leaving him there to think. Too much.

She decided to head to the bedroom. She didn't want to bring too much attention to her feelings of thinking that NaCharles wasn't 100 percent with this plan, not like the other ones. She paced the bedroom, cell phone in hand, ready to call Enoch. She put light pressure on the green button and quickly changed her mind. She and NaCharles had been through so much together. From the day she met him, she had lied to him about her age and where she was from, about her real job, and all the crimes she'd committed. He was so naïve—such a minor. She had been nothing but deceitful from the time she'd first spoken to him . . . all the way up to twelve hours before their last run. He was so innocent, and he adored her. Her thoughts drifted.

"Gosh, you're gorgeous, Pooh." NaCharles rubbed his hands lightly across Masha's face. She blushed like a typical teenager as he put both of his hands in hers.

"That's so sweet." Masha led NaCharles to her bedroom. She wanted to be sure to get him on her side while he was yet young and naïve and vulnerable and madly in love with her.

"NaCh, I need your help. I have to get my money back from a bad man. I worked so hard to earn my money to take care of us. Can you help me?"

NaCharles' blood boiled. Who would take money from such a lovely creature? Masha explained in her own version how a bad man supposedly took her money. NaCharles couldn't have been older than sixteen at the time. He looked older with his full young adult beard and his height only enhanced the effect. Masha loved that about him. She tried to remember the last time she told a boy she was younger than eighteen when she was twenty-four. They couldn't see past her beauty. Now here stood this young boy ready to commit crimes in the sad name of love. She chuckled to herself and continued the charade. It had worked perfectly several years ago. Today, Masha wasn't so sure that it would work now. She stood in the middle of the bedroom. NaCharles remained, staring out of the kitchen window.

Enoch wouldn't be pleased if either Masha or NaCharles failed to take the diamonds and money. No one was to get hurt, and she was instructed not to tell NaCharles too much. Only that it was the last run. Take the diamonds and money from Spints. She remembered how NaCharles' face lit up at the sound of "the last run". It would then just be him and her. The problem with the whole plan was that they were to take the money and diamonds from Spints. What worried Masha was that NaCharles wasn't wooing her as much. In all the time she'd known him, he didn't ask a lot of questions, but he was always so overly genuinely loving toward her. It was their "last run" she wanted to remind him once more. Masha knew that there would probably be some bloodshed but, whose? Precocious

While Masha paced the bedroom, NaCharles stared out the window, contemplating his own next steps. His mother had always told him to make better decisions. He thought more about his decision-making . . .

The fire alarm screamed as the staff shouted exit instructions. NaCharles laughed as the students exited the building in different emotional states—frantic, frustrated, and some a bit scared. NaCharles slipped away from Mrs. Pointington and headed for the boys' restroom. He would spice things up a bit when it came time for the accountability of the class. He wished he could be there to see the look on his teacher's face when she discovered he was not with the rest of the class.

It was an awful day for Mrs. Pointington and NaCharles. But NaCharles had no care that she was suspended without pay and he was up for expulsion. He laughed to himself as he waited in the principal's office for his parents.

His mother had been right. He needed to start making better decisions. He silently vowed that he would make better decisions right after he completed this "last job" for Masha. By that time, Masha had returned to the kitchen to join him at the window. As she stood next to him, she immediately confirmed that she'd sensed something was out of place.

NaCharles was involved. Detective Richard Larry Wingsong called Standford to confirm that NaCharles was a positive identification. The last run had turned fatal or near-fatal according to Detective Richard Larry Wingsong. The court date was set for August 15 at 3 p.m. NaCharles would remain in police custody until his court date. They watched and tried not to cry too loudly as their only child was whisked away by two uncaring policemen, a set of unforgiving chains, and an unbiased bailiff. It wasn't his fault that he had to be so unsympathetic to their situation. She knew at that moment that it was good that she and Ninx had come together to support their son. In the courtroom, Standford had stood on weak legs as she pushed her mind back to another day like this one. In her mind, her tears flowed freely; though it was NaCharles this time, it was her all over again. She thought about the time . . .

"Standford, if you don't get yourself together, God will do it for you. I know, I know," her mom said before Standford could inject, "you're thinking this is a bunch of crock, and maybe it is. I just don't want you to have to regret your young adult decisions for the rest of your life."

Stanford knew full well that her mother was right, but something told her that her mother had it all wrong. She'd learned at church that God is good all the time and that she was a child of God. Who doesn't take care of their child? Yes, Mom was all wrong; a bad decision wouldn't kill her. And it didn't. It *did*, however, send her to an adult prison for three years. Standford spent three years of her young adult life in a hardcore prison for women. When she was released at age twenty-two, she vowed to never return and to make sure no one from her family—especially her children—didn't experience it.

On the appointed court date, Standford watched as the judge took her seat. She was young, pretty, and didn't look at all like her image of a typical judge. Ninx, Standford, and NaCharles remained standing. NaCharles looked eleven years old again, and Standford was overcome by the situation. Ninx didn't know or understand. He'd always been an upright young man and an excellent father. Had their youth caused them to separate? Had their inability to raise their son caused their separation? She didn't know which reason to hold on to as the real reason.

Stanford promised to be strong regardless of the judge's ruling. *"All things work together for good,"* she repeated to herself. She could hear her mother mouth those same words twenty-seven years before today. She'd been seventeen, and here she stood at age forty-four, mouthing the words for her son who was only twenty-three.

She and Ninx met at church. After she was released from prison, she promised her parents that she would get her life together. There was a special Friday Night service. As promised, Standford went with her parents. The small church was filled from front to rear. Standford could feel the love as soon as she walked into the church. The mothers hugged and kissed her as she passed them. She could hear the whispers that she was an angel, lovely, blessed. Standford smiled as she made her way to a seat. Prison was tough. She was glad to be alive. As she followed her mother to a seat, her eyes met Ninx's. What a handsome young man! Suddenly, she was really glad she had come. She knew she couldn't ask her mother who he was, and she didn't know anyone else there. She wasn't sure what storyline her parents gave as an explanation of her prolonged absence. It wasn't like she'd been attending on a regular basis and then stopped. She hadn't stepped inside a church since age fourteen. Her parents pleaded with her but, she saw no use. She loved her parents, and she loved what she was doing even more.

The service was lively. Standford would know no difference. The lady at the podium introduced Devesta Morris to sing a solo. Her mother rose from her seat with one of those matching dress suits with a nest of a hat. Tonight, she wore the cherry-red blazer and knee-length skirt and the black hat with all sorts of feathers coming out of it. She sat in front of four people who struggled to get a nice view of the pulpit. When she went from her seat to go sing, the four members seemed relieved and began whispering, perhaps hoping she didn't return. They probably wished she'd take a seat on one of the side pews near the deacons and where the ministers' wives sat each Sunday, donning their pot-sized hats as well.

Standford realized she'd missed so much before and during prison that she had never heard her mother sing "I Told the Storm." There wasn't a dry eye in the place. Standford's tears were from the memory of her childhood, which could have been better coupled with her mother's angelic voice.

She felt the tears form on her cheeks as she tried to focus on the court proceedings. She could hear herself crying for her son yet focusing on the memory of her mother's song. She could hear the song so clearly, although it was so long ago. And today, she sat in a courtroom similar to the one she sat in to hear her own sentencing.

The preacher took the podium fashioning straight shoulder-length hair. Unusual for a preacher. Standford pretended to pay close attention while trying to glance over at the young man sitting in the left set of pews. She was sure he was paying attention, and she was sure she was paying attention to him paying attention. The preacher wore a light pink dress shirt with a soft grey bowtie. She thought him a bit too old for a pink shirt and when did pink become a man's new black? And what was with all that hair? Too long in prison. The bowtie was wrapped neatly around the preacher's neck with fake diamonds on either side. His matching grey blazer fit snugly against his broad arms, shoulders, and small waist. The outfit looked uncomfortable, but the preacher stepped forward in slow motion with much ease and confidence. He tapped the mouthpiece of the microphone followed by, "Faithfulness to Jesus," in almost a whisper. The church seemed too quiet. All had their eyes on him.

The congregation was captivated. He wore a large ring on each finger, and one could see the single women trying to determine if the one on his left index finger was a wedding band or just another large ring. He scanned the crowd. Standford watched his eyes, which landed upon the young man that she'd just had her eyes on just minutes before. She quickly faced front after realizing she'd turned almost completely around following the preacher.

"Faithfulness to Jesus. Saints, this world is broken. It's not like God intended for it to be. For those of you who are here for the first time, my name is Pastor Curthersby Oliver Nathan Walshburn III." Standford almost burst into laughter. Long hair, long name, who'd have thought? She gathered her composure in time for him to blurt out, "Turn with me to Ephesians chapter three."

Standford had thoughts turning in her mind as the Bible pages rustled to the chapter. At that moment, she knew she'd returned to where she was and how she had ended up in prison. I desire that ye faint not at my tribulations . . . which is your glory.

She was almost ready to accept NaCharles' fate but just couldn't bring herself to accept what would happen. She looked up to read the name of the judge. The placard read "Judge Casey George"—nothing like Pastor Curthersby or Oliver Nathan Walshburn III. With a name like Casey George and a face of a Hollywood star, NaCharles would surely serve hard time, or she'd be lenient. She just couldn't tell. She almost wished that NaCharles could look more like Ninx. Nonetheless, time would be done.

NaCharles was handsome enough, but Judge Casey George was too beautiful, and she would definitely get her way. The small group of spectators took their seat at the instruction of the bailiff. Ninx took Standford's hand. She could hear him whisper a short prayer. An emergency prayer. The courtroom seemed to grow too quiet. Standford stilled her hand in Ninx's large warm hand. She wanted to cry out, asking God to please have mercy on her son. She could hear herself reminding God that he was only a child. She begged for forgiveness. She had learned about intercessory prayer. She stood, requesting on her son's behalf. She managed to look over at NaCharles. He held no readable expression. What she didn't know was that he was crying so hard inside that his face showed no sign of physical emotion. He still couldn't believe that Masha, the love of his life, would put his and another man's life in danger. And all for what? He didn't want to look at his father, although he knew he wouldn't judge him. He couldn't look at his mother. His heart hurt for her because she told him about her time in prison and that it was her motherly duty that he never go to prison. He was angry with himself that he'd let her down—that it had come to this day. He then thought about Masha. He couldn't look at her for support and courage because she wasn't there. He thought of all her promises to him. His heart cried uncontrollably. He wanted to be a man that he really wasn't which caused him to wear such a hard face to cover his aching heart.

"We have to be on one accord," Stanford pleaded in a whisper as she held out her hand toward NaCharles, who seemed to be out of her reach. There were no tears, no expressions of sadness, nothing. Standford wasn't sure if she was comfortable with his apparent lack of emotions. She looked over to Ninx, who seemed to wear a "let God do His thing" expression. She searched her mind for comfort and immediate peace of mind, finding neither regarding her current situation. The time seemed to drag on forever as they waited for the definite sentencing or miraculous acquittal. Standford looked at NaCharles again and felt a soft touch on her shoulders. Everyone was seated except her. Ninx guided her to her seat. Her heart was heavy, and her soul ached.

Memories of her own childhood flooded her mind. The unnecessary stress she'd put on her parents; it all seemed so unfair in the moment, but she knew her son would likely suffer the sins of his mother. From her brief church attendance, she understood God to be a righteous and forgiving God. She also learned that we have a chance and we reap what we sow, for better or worse. She chose to do unpleasant things from her teenage to young-adult years, sowing bad. She'd accepted her trials and consequences. NaCharles was her baby, and she had the responsibility to be there for him like her parents had been there for her. She chose to sow the bad things and now she regretted those actions.

As she forced her heart and mind to clear, understanding and knowing that God is still good, she took her seat, ready to accept NaCharles' trial. For the second time in her life, she made another vow: *"God, whatever Your will is this day, please, please be with me and my baby—and my husband—on our journey from this trial to, I know and trust, a triumph."* She said "husband" although they had been separated and officially divorced for almost seven years. That was a prayer for another time. She dried the remaining tears, still wondering for the moment why she said husband and not ex-husband or NaCharles' father. She did know that God understood.

Judge Casey shifted the papers. The courtroom was very quiet. Standford had begged her parents and relatives not to come. It was hard enough for her to maintain a calm demeanor hearing the final decision. She mentally practiced bracing herself and accepting whatever the judge decided. In reality, she didn't know how she'd actually react. Her reaction could result in her and NaCharles *both* facing time. A *long* time. Yes, it was a good decision coming with only Ninx. He was still the love of her life. He was still a patient man waiting and trusting in God. His love for her was unwavering; she always knew that. Ninx was so God-like in his actions. The love that she now realized or admitted that she'd ruined sitting in the midst of her son's freedom being jeopardized made her feel worse. She began to blame herself. She was the reason for their irreconcilable differences. Her safe excuse. Had she done as God instructed, they wouldn't be here today. "That's how we got here," she sobbed into her hands. Ninx rubbed her shoulders to calm her. Now she felt compelled to ask for his forgiveness. He'd make sure she remained calm and respectful. He was a good man of godly character. She had heard of the importance of character at church and let her mind take her there briefly.

"Today I will preach or should I say speak to you about character study. Genesis 13:8–10 talks to us about character. Let there be no strife, for we are brethren. The story of Abram and the herdsman talks about character. Abram suggested for Lot to go left and he'd go right; issue resolved. Lot would simply go to the left. Character is everything when it comes to living for Christ."

A hot Sunday morning. The air conditioning unit couldn't keep the church comfortably cool. Nonetheless, the congregation was in full force and quiet with attention as the preacher spoke to them about character. Standford thought about her and Ninx and her character when they argued; he called them deep discussions. Such a gentleman. It was an outright argument at best and she wanted to win. She'd put on an exaggerated show, shouting to get her point across. Ninx, on the contrary, was soft-spoken and genuinely cared about her emotions. She hated his calm, which caused her to shout louder and say ridiculous things. Yet, he still maintained a calm demeanor. Good character.

The preacher stood for a moment to the left of the pulpit. Standford knew he was about to share a rehearsed analogy. His crisp baby-blue suit did wonders for his character; a confident individual. Four buttons lay in a neat row on one side of the vest and one lone button on the other side. The black dress shirt and peach tie made the baby blue too bright for the atmosphere. There he stood, full of confidence, vigor, and unmatched character. His words fell upon the congregation like a soft blanket. His tone was like the perfect cooling temperature on a blistering hot day. He straightened his peach tie and continued.

"Lot took Abram's suggestion into consideration. He looked about the portion of land offered to him. Thought about it for not too long. Lot journeyed east. Abram west. They separated themselves one from one another. In today's terms, problem solved—by men of great character." The preacher adjusted his peach tie again and smiled at the congregation. His soft-toned confidence blanketed the front row. "Saints Abram and Lot didn't argue over who would do what. Let's put that in today's context. We have an issue with a co-worker or family member. Instead of resolving it like people of character, we like to make a scene. We protest, say ugly words, block the highway, stand in front of reputable businesses, lie in the middle of the shopping malls, destroy our own possessions. We don't take the time to think about how our character can affect others." He stopped and held his finger to his chin before saying his next words. "What if Jesus had no spiritual character? Where would that leave us?" He waited, then quickly announced, "In a mess. That's where."

The preacher tapped on his Bible, and a few deacons stood as if on command. The preacher's aide handed him a glass of water. He took a few sips, tapped his Bible again, and looked out into the congregation—a gentle toss of the blanket. "Character saints. Now let's see how your character lines up with tithes. Deacons." There were a few chuckles from the congregation. Probably from those who actually pay their tithes and give an offering. The preacher took his Bible and sat in the middle chair. The deacons went to the offering trays. The choir stood to sing. Standford smiled at Ninx. "Character study," she whispered.

Standford let her hand stay settled in Ninx's. She closed her eyes and lost her thoughts to words of prayer. She wanted it all to be over, but she loved her son and her now ex-husband whom she just realized she still needed. She mouthed "Why?" Ninx seemed to have heard her and looked in her direction briefly. She could feel his love and warm heart. She'd ask if they could try again since she felt that they still loved each other. A lot seemed to have happened in the time of their separation and divorce. She looked up to see the judge pounding her gavel. The people took their seats as directed. What had she missed?

"People, I understand that this young man was involved in a crime he had no intention of committing. But keep in mind that his choices almost cost the life of another man, and that we cannot have. Steven Mulberry may not ever be the same because of the actions of the young man seated before us." Judge Casey looked in the direction of the Mon family, pressing her eyes extra hard at NaCharles. Standford felt her skin crawl while Ninx took all the blame for each of them. Such a man of character. She couldn't blame Judge Casey, for if it were her and NaCharles Mon was fighting for his life because of the selfish actions of another person, she would have embraced the notion of punishing the perpetrator. Judge Casey continued in an obvious angry whisper while still pressing her hard, unsympathetic glare. "Steven Mulberry may even *die* because of the poor *selfish* choices of the young man seated before us." She was sure to emphasize the words *die* and *selfish*. "I have raised my own sons and wished them the best and prayed for them daily, always reminding them to make choices that will benefit them. Looking at Mr. and Mrs. Mon, I'm certain that they asked their son to do the same. It's unfortunate that he did not."

Standford flinched at the sound of the judge's voice and the use of her name. She'd heard all of this before when her parents sat in a similar situation while a judge read off her sentence to prison. She looked to see that NaCharles still wore no emotion on his face, sitting very still. Standford wanted to jump up and tell the courtroom that her son was a good boy and that he had just made one horrible decision. She felt her legs tremble listening to the judge tell the truth; as ugly as it was, it was still the truth: a very horrible selfish decision. She was in full agreement with the judge's position concerning Steven Mulberry. There was unbearable silence.

Standford could feel the sweat forming in her palms. Ninx was calm and collected. The other people in the courtroom were completely silent. Standford could feel the strength gradually leaving her legs. It had been a long journey worrying about what NaCharles was into next. The early-morning phone call two weeks prior had shaken her soul. Could there really be a triumph from this trial? It frightened her that NaCharles' face was still without emotion. She tried to tell herself that he had good reason.

The preacher was short but stood tall with confidence. The family was at a visiting church. Ninx, Standford, and NaCharles sat across from Mr. and Mrs. Derrick Morris. Derrick wore his favorite grey suit with the crooked buttons. He had on a dark-blue shirt that looked out of place on his neck. Mrs. Morris wore what seemed like a matching dress suit. They still looked elegant together. Standford was happy she came. All eyes and ears were on the preacher. The preacher stepped forward with his large Bible held in both hands. He paused for a second, then spoke. "You've probably heard of the story of Abram. You probably know the story of how and why God changed his name. You're probably aware of the patience that Abram endured to get to the level of success he enjoyed. God had promised to make him a father and a great man."

The verdict was read. Standford couldn't remember if she cried or screamed. She would need the patience of Abraham to get through her son's prison time. The background conversation silenced in her mind as she tried to decipher the verdict. She wasn't sure if Ninx was holding her or if she was still slumped in her chair. She tried to collect her thoughts to remember if Steven Mulberry had died or was fighting for his life. She struggled to understand if she heard the judge say seventy years, seventeen years, or seven years. Her ears were ringing and her heart was too heavy to stand.

"Stan, it's over for right now. We'll make it through. God's promise says so. I need for you to trust God on this one. He has a reason. We don't know what it is yet. He will tell us. Seven years isn't a real long time. We'll make it."

"Seven years?" Standford managed to ask. She could see his tears through his barrier.

"Yes, seven."

She missed her husband's strength and calm. She lifted her hands to dry his face. He cried but she also knew he trusted God in all things. She thought about Abraham and his request for a child. He had waited. Even though he and Sarah got a bit impatient. In the end, he waited. He waited a long time for God's promises. She remembered like it was last night.

"Abraham was ninety-nine years old at the time. God told him to pack up and go west because He was going to make him a great nation. God trusted Abraham, and it was obvious that Abraham trusted God. He told Abraham that he would have a great nation. Turn to Genesis 17:1–21."

As the Bible pages rustled, the preacher continued to tell the story of Abraham's journey to greatness. "Abram was told to change his name to Abraham. Remember, he only went by Abram. He was told he and Sarah would have a son. Sarah was ninety years old!"

The mothers waved and laughed quietly. Standford could hear the ladies whispering, "That's pretty old for child-bearing."

God was determined to work a miracle, and Abraham and Sarah would wait. Standford learned that Abraham waited for twenty-four years! He and Sarah were given a son. Twenty-four years.

Standford looked at Ninx and tried to smile. "If Abraham can wait on the promises of God for twenty-four years, surely we can wait seven." She just hoped that her patience and trust could be in deed as it was in words. She needed to hold on to the hands of God right then, and she thought about what kind of God she truly served.

Her mind strayed to another time . . .

"God is a coming-down kind of God. Remember verse two says God Almighty came down and revealed Himself. Abraham went through some changes—his name, his wife's name, his character, his family dynamics, his purpose, and then his desire."

The congregation was quiet. Standford looked at Ninx, who was totally attentive. The preacher went verse by verse, discussing, teaching, preaching about the changes. Telling about what patience could get you. Abraham waited on God to do His will. She learned that Abraham's family and faith changed them for the better. His patience or his increased patience helped him through his hard times. His obedience to God helped him to understand that all those events had to take place to get him to the leader of a Nation he eventually became. Standford whispered to Ninx, "Twenty-four years. Wow!" He smiled at her and returned his attention to the preacher.

In the courtroom, Ninx and Standford cried and held each other. Standford reached for NaCharles, who slightly leaned away. She understood the devastation, especially given the fact that Masha didn't even show up for any of the trial. She let her hand find comfort on Ninx's back. She didn't hold anything against her only child. Their journey was just beginning. NaCharles was given three days to get his business in order and report to prison to begin his seven-year sentence. What significance there was in the situation; three days and Christ rose. Seven years and God had the Earth created. Significance in numbers. Seven is God's number of completion. Something good has to come of this. Standford quietly prayed for the strength of Abraham, the patience of Job, and the love of David.

CHAPTER 2

The Verdict

He replayed the picture of his parents as they both stood holding each other listening to the reading and the sentencing; her legs gave way. In minutes, the courtroom slowly emptied. They were allowed to stay embraced for a moment longer. He didn't join them. They agreed the verdict was fair given the circumstances. It could have been harsher. There was some relief as there was a death attempt placed on a man's life. Seven years to . . .

The prison floor felt nothing like the warm bed NaCharles had shared with Masha for several years. He refused to replay in his mind the mistake that cost him his freedom. He tried to remember all the words the judge had spoken. He remembered her being beautiful. His handsome eyes and structured cheekbones did nothing for his case. The judge barely looked at him. He wasn't surprised that she didn't melt at him like several girls his age and older did when they saw him. When he spoke, it sent them into a frenzy of sick love. He tried to remember if Masha had done the same thing when they met. Evidently not. Masha didn't melt. She selected him for a specific purpose. Had she melted and gone into a sick frenzy, he probably wouldn't be standing in a cold cell for the next . . . he couldn't remember the number of years the judge had given him. He thought about his parents for the first time in a long time. His mother was such an angel of God, and his father stood strong through all his ordeals. Even the one three days ago. He had enjoyed his parents for that short time. He tried to remember when they were happy with each other. He tried to remember when he had done what they asked of him. His mother and father didn't disapprove of Masha; they just wanted him to consider his actions. Well, his *mother* totally disapproved and gave her reasons why. He hadn't listened, and it cost him his freedom . . . and their relationship. He tried to recall if they were still happy. His father promised to visit him in prison and that they would get through this. He promised to bring his mother on every visit, whether she talked or not. She'd be there. He knew his father would do just as he promised. He was a man of his word. A man of character. *Get through this.* He pondered his father's words. Did that mean his mother too?

It was the loveliest three days he'd enjoyed in a long time. He secretly hoped his demise would bring his parents back together. He needed to be strong for them. Be a man. How many years had the judge said? He wanted to ask his father but didn't want to ruin the moment. Those days were such a blur. When he reported they would tell him his sentence as a reminder and to make him feel bad about Steven Mulberry who was right now trying to come out of a coma.

NaCharles took the three days to think about how he had gotten where he was. He had done some not-so-good things but was always able to get off because of a technicality or his age. Masha had used him and his age to her advantage. *"You're a minor, NaCh. Nothing will happen to you. You won't do any hard time. Heck, you may not do any time!"*

The guard yelled, "Lights out prisoners!" startling NaCharles out of his daydream. The lights went out, and NaCharles started crying like a child.

"Seven, he whispered. The judge said seven years." Immediately NaCharles realized that he had done an awful thing from hooking up with Masha to trying to steal from a major drug king and watching the shooting of a young man nearly—doing nothing to help as the man almost died. He remembered Masha telling him again, "You're a minor. Nothing will happen to you."

Before he could tell her that he celebrated his eighteenth birthday five years ago, she'd already kissed him, placed the revolver in his hands, and told him to meet her at the pickup point. He cried into the empty streets, "Masha, I'm twenty-three years old and you know that!"

Steven Mulberry lay lifeless on the concrete. Blood started oozing from his ears. He didn't hear the sirens. He cried into the rough pillow. This would be his home for the next seven years. He lay in the darkness thinking about his dark moments. He could hear his grandmother explaining to him that he should always make an effort to do the right thing. She was right every time.

Standford stepped into the empty house, which suddenly felt too big and lonely. She longed for Ninx to stay the night but their chemistry was saying otherwise. Ninx wanted to stay but decided that tonight wasn't a good time to be with her. She could see the decision in his eyes. She cried inside but she did understand. She knew he wasn't seeing anyone. It wasn't his character. If he was seeing anyone, he would have told her so. That was his nature. He was such a man of Godly character that dating wouldn't be one of his plans despite being divorced. Standford was almost certain that he'd try to make it work with them before he took on the task of dating someone. She watched his chest go up and down slowly as he contemplated what to say and how they would go about dealing with NaCharles' unfortunate situation. In the doorframe, she noticed that Ninx was wearing her favorite dress shirt; blue with small red dots. She purchased it from Macy's for his birthday. He had it accessorized with a brown French-cut blazer. She watched him for a moment, wondering what had really happened to their marriage. She shifted her glance to see that he was wearing—brown slacks to match the blazer. She could see the form of his muscled thighs. She brought her attention back to their child's current situation. Before she closed the door, he gently took her hand and asked if they could talk about the situation for a moment. She consumed the darkness and broke down and cried. He guided her into the house, and they found their way to the couch.

"We'll need to go see NaCharles every week or at least every other week. What is a good day for you?" He waited for her to respond in the darkness. She felt fragile and he wanted to take her in his arms and kiss her forever. She watched his lips move but didn't hear the words. The good man that he was, he knew to repeat the question. "Stan, what is a good day for you to go with me to visit our son in prison?" He knew the words stung like bees. He also knew he had to ask. Standford mumbled, "Wednesday is a good day for me. You know I don't want to go. What will I say to him?" She sobbed into her hands. He took them and led her face to his shoulder. "You don't have to say anything. Just be there for us."

She knew he'd promised NaCharles, and she didn't want to let either of them down. "Okay. I'll go, Ninx. I'll go for us." They held each other for hours in the dimly-lit family room.

She watched him walk slowly to the car. He glanced up from the driver's seat, blew her an affectionate air kiss, and pulled away. She closed herself in the darkness of her house to continue her sadness and begin her new journey. Seven years. Where had all the time gone? How would she and Ninx and NaCharles survive for seven years? She cried and laughed at the same time as she remembered that seven is God's number of completion. She felt far from complete.

Her mind wandered . . .

The preacher had a soft voice, which comforted the congregation. Standford held on to Ninx's warm hand, listening intently to the preacher.

"Go with me to Mark chapter one and we will read verses 1–7 and then verse 9. All rise if you can and if you are able." The soft-spoken preacher waited as the saints stood. He walked away from the pulpit and held out his hand as he quoted the scriptures. "In the beginning . . . of Jesus Christ . . . my messenger shall prepare thy way . . ." He paused and looked about the congregation. Standford tried to grasp the meaning. She rearranged the sleeves of her blouse and adjusted her scarf. She squinted at the preacher and then her Bible as if she couldn't see the meaning from both.

The preacher said in an almost whisper, "The body, the dove, the messenger. And you thought you had it bad. After Jesus was baptized, He was marked by the dove from heaven to symbolize that He is the One True Son of God. His Spirit became one with God. Then, long after that, He was tempted for forty days and forty nights; He was in what we want to refer to as a different, uncomfortable situation." The golden tassels that dangled from each sleeve of the pastor's olive-green robe were hypnotic. The embroidered gold letters on the right spelled out Pastor Minoas. Standford was further confused about the body, the dove, and the messenger. She watched Pastor Minoas and the olive-green robe move about the pulpit, the tassels making a rhythmic clinking sound as they hit each other and the sides of the pulpit.

Standford could feel the hot tears rolling down her face. She wasn't sure if she was still standing by the window in her home or sitting on the pew at Friends Fellowshipping Together Church many years ago. The realness of the memory was so depressing yet so comforting that she stayed in it. She strained to remember Pastor Minoas' strong words spoken in his soft voice.

"Temptation is common to man just in case you didn't know. It is, folks." There were small chuckles from the congregation. Standford looked around to see that Sis. Chester hadn't cracked a smile. Standford leaned back and reminded herself not to ever get that bitter. Pastor Minoas continued, "If you walk with me to James and go to verse thirteen of the first chapter, you'll sort of understand my point. Let's walk there." He waited for pages to stop rustling and fingers to pause on iPads. He looked about the congregation. His tassels made uncoordinated beats on the sides of the pulpit. Then, he continued, "Let no man say . . . I am tempted by God. God doesn't just tempt. He has a purpose. Everything He does has purpose. Your life has purpose, and all that happens to you, good or bad, has a meaning." The preacher looked around as if someone had shouted out a wrong answer.

Standford looked about to see where he was looking. Ninx remained focused. She reached for his hand, and he took his eyes off her to look at her Bible.

"Luke 4:1 and 5 comes to mind," the preacher finally said. His olive-green robe set smoothly on his narrow shoulders. She could see the rise and fall of his name written on the chest part of the robe. He suddenly appeared a lot younger-looking than when the sermon began. Standford slowly turned to the book of St. Luke and read to herself . . . Jesus . . . full of the Holy Ghost . . . was led by the Spirit. Then the Devil took Him into the mountains and promised Him all the world if He worshipped him. Standford was familiar with the story. She tuned out after hearing the three points: Lust of the flesh. Lust with the eyes. Pride of life. In the face of temptation, call on the name of the Lord.

She still felt the sting in her heart, but the tears had dried. She looked about her home to see much time had passed since returning from the courtroom. She thought about all the so-called "fun" she was having so many years ago and how all that fun had cost her son's freedom. She had been tempted and given in to temptation instead of calling on the name of the Lord, and she knew that she was to call on Him. Her mother and father reminded her many times to trust in God and yield not to the temptations of the world. She thought she had, but now she realized she had simply pretended so she could do what she wanted instead.

The day had been a long one, and the night would be even longer—and seven years even longer. She walked through the house with familiarity. She walked in the darkness with ease and went to her refrigerator, not knowing what exactly she wanted; a sandwich, water, or a drink. She lifted the bottle of orange juice and bypassed the Vodka as she crossed the kitchen to the counter. How easy it was for her to push aside the temptation to drink away the sorrows she now felt. She wondered for a brief moment how NaCharles was doing in prison. He'd supposedly killed a man or attempted to kill him, she reminded herself. Her family would be changed, but that family would be changed forever.

She felt the tears form in her mind as she pictured her baby in a prison cell. Her heart ached, in reality, as she thought of the family

33

who had lost or had the possibility of losing their child too. Never to see him again, never see his children, never have a second chance for a loving moment. That family didn't have seven years. Standing in the darkness, she slowly poured a glass of juice, thinking of all the joy she had felt when her baby was born. She had smiled at him and Ninx, trying to think of a name that would mean something later. A special, unique name. There was so much in a person's name.

"What's in a name? What does a name mean?"

Standford took caution to sit next to the handsome young man she had seen at church last Sunday. Her mother and Dad had taken the empty seats two rows up. She was glad she'd worn a nice but tasteful dress. She only came to see if the handsome young man was there, and because she thought she'd get serious about getting her life together. She slid into the hard pew and listened to a sermon that she never thought she'd recall in later years.

"Turn with me to Genesis chapter seventeen, and let's read about what's in a name and think about why parents take special care when naming their children. Another point I want to make is the process of conception, as it relates to waiting on the promises of God."

There was a long pause. The congregation rustled in the pews, trying to understand. Standford felt like she already understood, so she opened the Bible she'd taken from the church pew pocket and began to read. Abram was ninety-nine years old . . . the Lord told him . . . thou shalt be a father and your name will now be Abraham. I will give unto thee . . . all the land of Canaan . . . This is my covenant. The young Standford read and understood that God blesses parents with children. She also, for some strange reason, understood those blessings come with waiting on the promises of God. She raised her head in time to hear the preacher say, "Wait on God's promise. Abram had to wait. In Genesis 17:16, God told Abram that Sarai, now Sarah, would bear a son and he would be a leader. When reading that scripture, one would think that Abram and Sarah had a baby boy and took over the nation in a short time. That was not the case. There were some sins committed, long-suffering in between, and a lot of time passed. They had to wait on the promises of God. The new names were given to them to start the process of change in their lives."

What's in a name?

God changed Abram's and Sarai's names to give them the special God treatment. She had named her baby NaCharles because his eyes told her that he would grow to be a great man with a gentle heart. He too would rule something and be someone. Now he had a prison number that would define him for the next seven years, but with patience, he could still be a great man with a gentle heart.

"What's in a number?"

The darkness consumed her metaphorically. She sipped more juice and headed off to settle for the night.

The lights flickered on and off until they stayed on for more than ten minutes. NaCharles jumped from the top bunk with ease. He also cried, realizing that he'd have to do that same gesture every day for the next seven years. Could his knees take it? His bunk mate stirred carelessly. NaCharles wanted to know how many years he had or at least how many he had served. He could hear the bar doors opening from the end. He gathered himself to exit the small cell. In his mind, he could smell Masha's fresh-mango hair. He suddenly missed her house. He thought of his parents and the weight of pressure on his mother. She had tried very hard to raise him to be a decent young man. And he *had* been a decent young man until he was tempted by Masha. He accepted that temptation. He resolved that his situation wasn't entirely her fault and he wouldn't make it her seven-year problem. NaCharles took his mind back to one of his grandmother's conversations regarding what was real and what was fake. Had he used what she taught him, he would still be a free man. Moreover, had he practiced then what he already knew, his life would be different. But he made the choices he made, knowing that he had very good and dedicated parents and extended support.

The bars opened on his end, and before he could step out into the internal freedom of the halls, his bunk mate grabbed him and pushed him so that he exited first. And here he thought the old man had rehabilitated from all the years he'd evidently served. NaCharles started to grab the old man and push him back into the cell but decided against it. Seven years was already long enough; making enemies within the first forty-eight hours would make the time even longer—and that much more dangerous. If he was going to prove his manhood, now wasn't the time to do so. He would take his time to learn who was with him and who wanted to see him dead for what he'd done that landed him in prison. He strained to remember if the man had died or was still in critical condition. The line between reality and his fantasies had begun to blur. He watched as Masha yelled at the young man. NaCharles remembered how lovely she looked even though the man pleaded for them to just take whatever they came for and leave. He had cried uncontrollably, begging for mercy because he had or planned to have a wife and child—or children. NaCharles only remembered lovely Masha in her black full-body suit and her face covered with a pink mask. Had the man lunged at her? He remembered shots were fired. He remembered Masha telling him that he was a minor and nothing would happen to him. Was the situation real? NaCharles slowly walked out of the cell, thinking about the reality he currently faced. He wasn't a minor and how hurtful it was to him that Masha didn't even remember. He let his mind drift . . .

The preacher was way too handsome to be a preacher. His burgundy shirt fit well on his shoulders, giving him an almost exotic look. He smiled, and the electricity of it filled the entire church. He paused at the edge of the podium, pointed his finger, and said, "Is it live or is it Memorex? Is it real or is it fake? Are you saved or are you not?"

NaCharles read the long sermon title inside the program the usher handed him when he entered the church. He looked about the massive church until his eyes locked on his father, who sat three pews from the front. NaCharles recognized his broad shoulders and smiled, happy to see him deep into the service as usual. Ninx was his father—a great man, loving, caring, and a true Christian. At such a young age, he knew his mother was loved. He knew Ninx loved him too. He taught him how to be a good kid and reminded him daily that it was important for him to grow up to be an excellent young man. NaCharles nodded his head and went to find a seat.

The handsome preacher had the congregation turn to Matthew 13:24–30. The pages quickly turned back and forth until the preacher began to read. His voice waved across the congregation sounding like a professional choir. He stood with his head in the Bible. He wore a black robe with white stripes on the sleeves. His right wrist donned a gold watch that looked like a Rolex. NaCharles was sure members complained about a $10,000 Rolex watch from a $4,000-a-month congregation. It didn't quite add up. Nonetheless, NaCharles, wanting to impress his father, used the church Bible and turned to the scripture and began reading along with the handsome preacher and his Rolex.

A man planted a garden. While he rested, bad men came and mixed the garden seeds with bad seeds. When the garden began to grow, it wasn't until well later that the man noticed he had bad seeds planted amongst his good crop. He instructed the servant to rip out the bad crop but realized that in doing so his good crops would be destroyed. He had to figure out a way to let the crops grow together and still benefit from the harvest. The farmer let the crops grow together. At harvest time, he safely separated the good crop from the bad crop.

"What do the tell-tale signs of your life point to? What is your reality and what is fake? The farmer didn't separate the wheat from the tares. At the time the seeds were planted, no one could tell which were the good seeds and which were the bad seeds. They all looked the same. However, as the seeds were cultivated, their true character showed and the farmer was able to tell the real plants from the fake plants. He told his servant the enemy had placed the bad seeds in his garden. Instead of destroying the crop trying to determine which was good and which was bad, he waited and let them all grow together. When it was time to harvest, the servant was able to clearly determine which to keep. What tell-tale signs let the servants know the "real" harvest from the "fake" harvest? What are the tale-tell signs of your life?"

NaCharles couldn't believe how clearly he remembered that sermon. Perhaps because the preacher was way too handsome. He even remembered all the young ladies trying to talk to him after the sermon. They probably didn't understand the scriptures. They probably didn't even know how to find the scriptures. They didn't even read the sermon title in the bulletin. He watched as each woman shook his hand way too long for church, held the hug way too long for a friendly greeting, and asked way too many unnecessary questions about the sermon as the fellowship line extended into the vestibule. He chuckled a little to himself and walked to the semi-freedom hall of the prison thinking that those ladies didn't even remember he mentioned that he had a wife just as Masha didn't remember that it had been years since his seventeenth birthday. He strolled along, knowing that he had to survive amongst the innocent criminals and the true criminals whether he could quickly tell the difference or not. No one could tell who was who until a situation broke out. He didn't want anyone to know that he was guilty of a possible attempted murder. He would mingle with the general population and try to look like and act like the wheat and not the tares.

As he reached the internal freedom hall, the smell of bondage and depression hit him immediately. The memory of his father listening attentively to the handsome preacher started to fade. Yes, seven years was way too long to deal with enemies. He'd grow with the wheat and the tares and wait until harvest time. He would be the greatest servant to survive, hoping God would have mercy on his current situation. He had to convert to wheat if he was to make it to harvest time.

"Okay ladies, you have one hour in the field, and then we have prison chores. Yes, ladies. How'd you think we keep this rat hole clean? It's not my home, and some of you'll be here a while, so we have to assign chores to our newcomers. You old-timers can keep the ones you have or trade with a newcomer." The skinny guard belted out the instructions with the voice of a linebacker. He stood about six feet but looked to weigh only 180 pounds at best. NaCharles returned his thoughts to the farmer's seeds. They all looked the same until they started to grow.

What were the tale-tell signs to know which was wheat and which was tares? This skinny young man was probably the strongest guard, but who would know until you crossed him? Just like it was hard for the farmer to tell what was wheat and what was tares by simply looking at the garden plot before him. The farmer had to wait. Looking at the skinny guard shouting out the demands for the day was similar. Evidently, no one had challenged the guard because they just didn't know. They hadn't judged, or they would have had an encounter and discovered he was a tare or a really good thread of wheat. NaCharles felt the need to return to the way-too-handsome preacher's sermon.

"God's judgment will separate the good from the bad."

In his reminiscence, NaCharles walked to the edge of the hall and waited in line to go outside for one hour. He almost started to cry when he realized that within three days, his life had been reduced to this. He looked around to see all the solemn and hard faces. He didn't know if he'd be the wheat or the tare; harvested or destroyed. He did know that he had to choose to be one or the other.

"Okay, inmates. You have only one hour. Play nice."

CHAPTER 3

Trusting God

T he pressure to give in to the inmate survival rules would soon come into play. He wasn't sure how to take it all in and continue to trust in God's promises. Tears begin to flow at the thought of his only son in prison without the tools needed to survive and maintain his young, manly dignity without the tools to trust in God of all things. Is true faith really built on difficult times? This test was close to . . .

Ninx pulled the shirt over his head to also dry his tears in the process. His only child, his son, NaCharles Mon, would be imprisoned for seven years. He walked slowly to the small closet to get his running shoes. He wanted to keep his life "normal" and on a routine but had struggled since the reading of the verdict. He saw his beautiful wife in his mind's eye. He had just left her on the porch of their home to make it through the night alone. He tried to remember why he didn't stay the night. Even in divorce, in the eyes of God, she was still his wife.

"Is this a new day?" he asked himself. Or had it just been several hours that passed since he pulled away from the curb of their home? He couldn't remember at the moment. He instead tried to remember why they had separated and had been divorced for almost seven years. Was this a trial of trust or punishment for sins he'd committed? The tears returned, flowing uncontrollably.

"What have I done for my son to deserve this?" He lifted his tear-filled eyes to heaven. "Please, God, tell me what can I do to undo this . . . or at least get us all through it." He still felt responsible for the health and well-being of his family. It was his job to raise his son properly and to support his wife. He felt like a failure as he held the blue and grey Nike cross-trainers, one in each hand, the green laces freely dangling on either side of the shoes. He gave them a little shake while making his request to God, "Please tell me what to do and then help me to do it the right way? My son is locked up and my wife is locked out. I need You to help turn these trials into triumphs. In Your Son Jesus' name, I stand humbly before you and pray. Amen."

He walked into the small bedroom to put on his shoes. The efficiency apartment suddenly felt smaller. He looked about the three rooms in one glance. When the divorce was final, he told Standford that he would move out and she was to stay in the house just in case their son wanted to be home. He looked at the small space from the bedroom across to the small bathroom that only held a shower, a sink, and a toilet. The ashen wallpaper screamed for a makeover. The tile was chipped at the base of the sink. He moved his gaze to the kitchen area, which he could also see from the bedroom. The microwave was an older version, but it worked fine—and *overtime*, heating up those boxed meals. Ninx hadn't been motivated to cook since he moved out when the divorce was official and final. He wanted something affordable that was close to Standford and his son. "I'm not going to go far, Standford, because we're going to make this work," he'd told her and promised in his heart. "Also, I want you to be able to contact me whenever you need me. I still love you and perhaps always will. You take the time you need to figure things out, and I'll do the same."

He sat on the full-size bed for several minutes. He cried again asking, "God, please help me to understand. Please. I don't understand but, I want, I need, to trust you."

Rising to his full height, the preacher stood at least seven feet tall. He towered over the small podium looking out over the congregation. Ninx had explained to Standford that this would be a tall night of spiritual excitement. Standford laughed. When they got to the church and she gazed upon the tall preacher, she laughed again at Ninx, who smiled warmly. The preacher was dressed more for a gala than a church event. His white tuxedo went well with the red dress shirt sporting a red, black, and white bowtie. He was wearing a pair of large black-rim glasses that set neatly on his hazel green eyes. He wore a bright large diamond ring on each middle finger. The ring on the left hand was either for show or a woman in the congregation really loved him. The thick gold necklace with the two-inch cross dangled freely as he moved. The preacher's armor-bearer was preparing him to bring a word from the Lord. The much shorter man set a glass of orange juice and a glass of water on the small table next to the podium. He placed the very large Bible on the podium and hung a white silk towel across his right shoulder.

Ninx and Standford moved quickly to the middle of the church as the crowd gathered in full force. Standford's parents had asked Ninx to take her and for them to be sure to arrive early to get good seats. They arrived just in time to get really good seats. Ninx felt like he was on a spiritual date with his wife of two years. She was so young and pretty and in need of a good word from the Lord, for both of them. She was even prettier pregnant. Ninx was scared to be a father, but he knew that he had to trust in God. His father reminded him daily to trust in God even when he didn't understand. They settled in their "really good" seats and waited for the service to begin.

The tall preacher stood at the podium while the choir sang a lovely opening song, "This Is Your Season." Ninx and Standford held hands and sang quietly with the choir.

"It's working for my good. It's good, real good. This is my season for grace for favor." They nodded with eyes closed and hearts clear. The choir was followed by a powerful prayer from a deacon who couldn't have been a day over thirty. The tall preacher still stood at the podium while all of this took place. Ninx looked at the way-too-young deacon and closed his eyes in respect for his position and to take in the prayer. Ninx prayed in a whisper, but his heart cried out loud. He wanted God to understand that he was bringing a child into the world and needed constant blessings and limitless mercy to get him from birth to

adulthood. He held Standford's hand gently, but his soul held her tight. The deacon finished the prayer, the choir sang two more selections and the tall preacher seemed to reclaim his position at the podium, dominating the pulpit.

The preacher now moved slowly about the pulpit as if taking in the atmosphere. Standford noticed that he had remained standing during the opening events, the choir, and of course the deacon's prayer. He looked as if he would sniff out those who needed to hear the Word of God. It wasn't a terrifying feeling but rather a feeling of sincerity, trust, and confidence. The seven-foot preacher projected confidence and spiritual energy. The silence seemed to stretch on forever, and then he spoke. His voice filled the church as a hush seemed to fall over the congregation. It was quiet. Very quiet.

"My wife of ten years gave birth to our twin daughters five years ago." The voice didn't seem to fit the fly attire he sported. His voice was humble and mesmerizing. The congregation was attentive.

"I was a proud father," he continued, "and I loved being a father. And you know how us men get when we have only daughters; we want sons or a son too. I wanted a son. I believe I harassed my wife for years until we got pregnant again and she indeed gave birth to a healthy baby boy. I was beside myself. I loved my daughters and I especially loved my son." He paused and looked about the congregation. He tugged gently on his red dress shirt. He adjusted his bow tie for no reason. The rings sent rays down the middle aisle. Ninx noticed that the sleeves were the right length for such a tall man. He looked well-groomed. Simply Godly. The congregation was still very quiet. Very quiet. The extra-tall preacher walked to the front of the podium.

In what sounded like a tense voice he said, "When he was ten years old, my only son fell ill. He was very sick. We took him to at least three doctors and got the same prognosis. He had a rare disease and wouldn't live to see his eleventh birthday. I was devastated. I was perhaps angrier than devastated—so much so I don't remember if I asked my wife if she needed my support. Looking back on the situation, I realize that was very selfish of me. I told God that He had blessed us with a son that

He would now take away too soon. My wife seemed to be strong, but I was never sure because I didn't ask her. Instead, I spent the next year in a verbal battle with God. How dare He take my only son. I didn't, couldn't, and wouldn't understand. I prayed the prayer of the century one night as my son lay in the children's hospital. He looked so fragile and helpless. I was mentally and spiritually weak—exhausted. I knew that God had forgiven me for all the things I had said and thought and did. I even accused *Him* of being selfish. *I* was selfish."

The preacher paused and held his head down as if praying. The congregation was on edge with suspense. Ninx felt tears spring from his eyes as he thought about his upcoming journey as a father. His child hadn't yet been born, and listening to this man tell his humbling, heart-wrenching story to a congregation of apparent strangers made him cry. Standford grab his hand and held it on her swollen belly and used her free hand to massage his back. She understood his emotions. He had promised over and over that he would be solely responsible for the proper rearing of their child—for the protection of his family.

The preacher lifted his head and continued. The congregation was still very quiet.

"Later in the night my son opened his eyes and called for me . . ." His voice quivered. "Of course, I rushed to his bedside trying to be strong for him. In that moment, so clearly, he asked me in his ten-and-a-half-year-old body, "Daddy, are you still going to trust God even when you don't understand?" I burst into tears. I couldn't control them. I had preached that sermon almost a year prior. My son, my only son, dying in the hospital asked me if I'd trust God even if I didn't understand! I was beside myself. Who'd think that a nine-year-old would listen that closely to a sermon? Saints, you can ask any one of those doctors and nurses and even my wife. Saints, I was full-blown in tears right there in the room, and my son was expecting an answer from me."

There wasn't a dry eye in the place. Some grown men were crying louder and harder than the women. There were even a few deacons trying to maintain some dignity but, one could see the tears streaming down their faces. The preacher knew that he must continue.

44

"Saints, please turn to Hebrews 11:17–19." The pages rustled slowly.

Ninx, Standford, and the entire congregation, except for the preacher's wife, turned their Bible pages, expecting to hear the end of the story. Ninx tried not to look over at the preacher's wife, but his curiosity got the best of him. He slowly glanced to see that she was stark still, Bible in hand with no apparent distraught look. She wasn't crying; she didn't look sad or angry—just still. She wore her long hair in a neat bun gathered to the left side. She had on a matching tuxedo dress with a red, black, and white scarf instead of a bow tie. She too wore a large diamond on both index fingers. She dabbed her cheeks of smearing makeup. Perhaps more so from the heat of the church, not because she was crying. She watched the tall preacher tell the story of her son. Their only son. *Truly a woman of great courage and strength*, Ninx thought as he returned his attention to the preacher.

Ninx asked in a whisper, "Had God saved their young son?" He couldn't tell from his wife's expression, which bore no traces of a response at all. The preacher turned his Bible a few pages and begin to speak. "Saints, my son passed away in the hospital two days before his eleventh birthday."

The weight of the suspense lingered in the air. Chocking sounds were heard throughout the building. Those who were quietly crying suddenly broke and begin crying out loud. The deacons nearly fell to their knees. There were only a few people present who knew that the son had died, and they still cried as if hearing the storying for the first time today.

The preacher was familiar with the reaction because he'd been there. As horrible as it sounded each time—and how his heart ached each time—he'd learned that God told him to tell the story each time so that people would understand. He could still feel that same knot in his stomach—just like on the day he saw his son take his last breath. He'd wished for a long time that he'd never preached about trusting in God no matter what.

The comfort teddy bear was still clutched in the crook of his son's left arm. The cords and tape dominated his small frame. The large hospital bed suddenly seemed to devour the boy and all of the bed's contents. The preacher couldn't hear the machine's alarm over his desperate cries. In his mind's eye, he remembered the reaction from his lovely wife. It looked insensitive at the time, but later, he realized that it was heroic trust in God.

He looked at his wife, who looked stoic and supportive, and continued.

"Saints, do you know a real hero when you see one?" Although it was rhetorical, he still looked about as if soliciting a response. "Well, I have seen one. I know one. Better yet, I live with one. When our son took his last breath in that hospital, I broke down completely. Look at me. I'm seven foot, 250 pounds. Look at how I'm dressed. Many of you know my personality and demeanor. Saints, I tell you as God is my witness, I wimped out, and I'm the one who's supposed to be the gatekeeper for my family! I know to trust in the Lord no matter what. I preach all the time to trust in the Lord. Yet, on that day, I lost trust. I became angry with God. I felt forsaken and forgotten. It was my only son. But . . ." The pause was awkwardly long yet necessary. "Thank God for my wife." He looked in her direction again while talking to the congregation. A smile strained across her face. He returned a smile.

"When the alarms started ringing and I started crying hysterically, I was able to hear my wife's words, and to this day, I can say them. She closed her eyes, raised her head and hands to Heaven, and this is what she said verbatim: '*Thank You, God, for our son and the time you gave us. Now please protect my baby's soul. I will continue to trust in You knowing that there is a job for us all. Our son is with You, and while he was with us here with my family, we loved him and You for giving him to us. Going forward, we can persevere but, we need strength. Thank you, God.*'

"Those were her exact words." He looked over to his wife who was nodding her head, but not a tear was to be seen. The congregation probably thought she was insensitive as well, but the preacher had explained that she was able to hear God and was ready for their next steps. He explained that she was able to trust God no matter what, and she trusted Him even when she didn't understand. The preacher gave her a loving smile, but all could see that he was still the weaker of the two as tears began to form in his eyes. As the tears begin to roll slowly down his cheeks, he immediately attempted to regain his composure and continued. "I was crying so hard, I couldn't hear God, but strangely, I could hear my wife's words, and to this day, I still remember them. I had preached about trusting in God no matter what. Trusting in God even when we don't understand. Never did I imagine that my only son would remember the words—the meaning of my sermon—and then use it at such a hard time in his life and mine.

"I was so hurt, Saints. I was mad at God. My wife and I almost divorced. And it would've been my fault alone. His last words to me were, 'Daddy . . . Are you still going to trust God even when you don't understand?'"

Ninx could hear the sniffles behind him. Mothers and grandmothers cried, but the preacher's wife shed no tears. None at all. Ninx tried to shield Standford from seeing the lack of emotion on the wife's face as the preacher continued softly with what sounded like renewed confidence. "Please don't cry, for my son is truly in a better place, and although I still hurt and miss him terribly, I do understand, and I still trust God. I can honestly tell you I wasn't spiritually ready that day. I will honestly say that I had to trust in God again and try to understand—neither of which was easy to do. But he, my son, was so right, and it hurt so much."

He paused, looking to the ceiling, his hands on the podium. His tuxedo seemed to have lost its flare for the occasion. He dabbed his eyes and took a sip of water. There was an awkward stillness throughout the church. It lingered for about two minutes. The preacher seemed lost in thought. He took his eyes from the ceiling and planted them on his wife. She nodded lightly and waved her hand as if to tell him that he must go on. He gave her that same loving smile and turned to the congregation. Those who knew him well understood.

47

The continued silence of the congregation brought the preacher back to the sermon. "Now I'm not going to stand before you and say it's easy or that it was easy for me. It's hard, and it was very hard for me." His voice still sounded a little shaky. It had been years since his son passed away, but the feelings were as fresh as the minute he'd taken his last breath. He smiled at his wife, and she nodded. Ninx could feel that the preacher had told this story several times and from his wife, he drew the strength to completely tell it and trust in God. He was to be the living witness that God must be trusted no matter what and especially when we don't understand.

Ninx held Standford's hand and touched her swollen belly. He too had to trust in God, *especially* when he didn't understand. Tears began to stream from his eyes.

Ninx put on his running shoes and laced them with some renewed vigor. He went outside and stretched. He took in the fresh air and began to run. He wasn't sure what he was to do, but he was sure of what he *had* to do. He ran the five miles to the home he had shared with Standford and NaCharles until the divorce—their home. He would have to reconcile with Standford if they were to ever get through the next seven years. He struggled to remember the reasons for their separation and subsequent divorce. Initially, neither of them had filed for divorce. Then, one day, he came home to see the divorce papers on the kitchen counter. He planned to argue and fight for them to stay together. NaCharles was getting into trouble almost every day. Ninx attributed it to their separation. The divorce would make things worse, he thought. He just didn't have the strength to fight. He'd tapped out, signed the papers, and allowed the divorce to be final. In retrospect, he wondered if that had been a huge mistake.

Gentle warmth blossomed in Ninx's breast, but he continued to run. He thought about how he had gotten to where he was and where would he go. He needed to trust God. Truly trust God with all his being. NaCharles wasn't dead but seven years could probably kill him just the same. His chest burned with fatigue, but he kept running. He needed the strength from God to get his family from their current trial to a triumph.

He strained to remember the second point of the tall preacher's message. The first point was to trust in God even when you don't understand. They had attended to hear the preacher on another Sunday. NaCharles had been born by then, and Ninx remembered how happy he was to be a new father. He remembered how he had gone back to hear the preacher in hopes of getting some indirect pointers on how to raise his son right. What was that second point? He continued to run while his mind drifted back to the sermon.

The tall preacher had another message from God. This time, Ninx and Standford sat with their bundle of joy sound asleep in her arms. He had begged NaCharles to allow them the time to hear the sermon, and it seemed that NaCharles was keeping up his end of the request. NaCharles looked so peaceful and innocent. The church was equally crowded. Ninx was sure to arrive early to get a seat in the middle. He found the near-perfect spot. He motioned Standford into one of the two spaces toward the middle of the church, and the two of them sat close to each other as the service began, NaCharles nestled peacefully in his mother's arms.

The Praise Team sang "Set the Atmosphere". He felt like the congregation was spiritually moved. As they settled into their seats, the preacher came forward. He appeared taller than before in his long black robe with a red cross on either side. The sleeves and hem were laced in thick red thread. He appeared to have a stronger presence than the last time they'd seen him. He was equally as confident as the unduly handsome preacher. Although the man hadn't spoken a word, Ninx was dead set that the voice of the preacher would ricochet throughout the church with a definite word from the Lord. He waited.

The preacher walked to the front of the podium and gave and looked upon the congregation benignly. Ninx matched the stare, determined to absorb a Word from the Lord that he could use forever. His heart smiled at the thought of all the blessings he had received up to this point—a lovely wife who loved him and a cute baby boy whom he loved dearly. God had been very good to them.

"What is faith? Many of us are asking all the time, what is faith? I know that each of you has a different response. And that's okay. I, too, had to learn the real meaning and action of faith." The preacher was very different from the time Ninx and Standford had heard him almost six months before. They smiled as they held their bundle and listened with hope and trust in their hearts.

"Now, you know that faith is action? Take a moment to think about the story of Shadrach, Meshach, and Abednego. That was faith in action. Truly, take a moment." The preacher silenced and stared in no particular direction as the congregation contemplated the three Hebrew boys, not men. They had been mere teenagers at the time.

The silence was sufficient. Ninx held his family close to his heart, and his soul cried a little as he did take the time to think about faith and how to exercise it. He even took a moment to think about the last time he heard the tall preacher talk about trusting God even when you didn't understand. Now he spoke about faith and action.

The preacher continued, and Ninx concluded that this preacher's presence was stronger than the handsome preacher they had heard more often.

"So, now that you've had time to think about faith, let me tell you my version of its definition. Faith: acting like a thing is so. Even if it ain't so. Because God said it's so. Let me say it again slowly." He took a breath and repeated the definition slowly, "Faith: acting like a thing is so. Even if it ain't so. Because God said it's so." He paused and continued, "Think about that. Faith is having the trust in God for something even if all the world deems it impossible. God makes it possible. No matter what. The 'no matter what' is where we lose sight of faith." He looked as if he'd forgotten to say something.

"Did I give the scripture for today's Word?" There were a few murmurs from the congregation. "Daniel 3:1–26. Now I'm not going to read the entire chapter, but I do want you to read it as spiritual homework. Like the teachers do, I'll give you a summary."

The preacher picked up his Bible and stepped to the left side of the podium. "Does everyone have the scripture?" He paused briefly and told the story.

"So, we have a mighty king who built a godly image. His instructions were that everybody, no exceptions, bow down and worship the image at the sound of the music; like a horn, short melody on a piano, or a guitar. Whatever the music, you bow. And those who didn't bow or in the Hebrew boys' case, *wouldn't* bow, would be placed in the fire. Now, we already know that every time instructions are given, there are always a few who just won't follow them. For whatever their reason, they refuse. I know that from my time spent in the Middle East. The music starts, and everyone is supposed to go to the mosque for prayer. One day, a few of my friends and I were at the mall, and the music began. When it started, stores closed, restaurants stopped serving, and all the locals and visiting Muslims would make their way to the nearest mosque to pray. Those were the directions given. I remember, one time, a man stopped to ask us if we wanted to buy carpet. So, clearly, following directions wasn't his priority. Making money was."

The congregation laughed, and spirits remained high as the preacher continued.

"So, at the appointed time, the music sounded, and all were to bow down. This went on a few times until the guards noticed that Shadrach, Meshach, and Abednego didn't bow. It probably went something like this: On Monday, the music sounded, and everybody bowed. Shadrach, Meshach, and Abednego didn't. The guards were like, 'Are they not bowing? Maybe they didn't hear the music. We'll give them that.' On Wednesday, the music sounded, and Shadrach, Meshach, and Abednego don't bow. The guards were like, 'Wait a minute; that music was loud today, and they didn't even try to bow.' And one of them probably said, 'And they're just teenagers acting like grown-ups. We need to take them to the king.' The guards stumbled over themselves to get to the boys. The conversation went like this:

"'Hey, you three. What're your names?'

51

"'Shadrach.'

"'Meshach.'

"'Abednego.'

"'Well, Shadrach, Meshach and Abednego did you hear the music?'

"They replied, 'Yes, we did.'

"'Then why did you not bow?'

"They probably replied with, 'That statue is not our God. We only bow to and for God, not a mass of stone.'

"This was not what the guard wanted to hear, and he wasn't happy with their response. 'Come, I must take you to the king.'

"Abednego probably mumbled, 'And.'"

The congregation laughed.

"Saints, you know it's always one. The guard escorted Shadrach, Meshach, and Abednego to the king.

"The king was in his castle sitting on the throne and said, 'Who are they and what's this all about guards?'

"The guards proceeded to talk all at once. The king raised his hand to silence them. 'Okay just one of you, please tell me the problem and why are there three boys with you?'

"The guard told the king that he was almost certain that when the music sounded on Monday, Shadrach, Meshach, and Abednego hadn't bowed. He said that he wasn't sure, so he waited to watch them today. 'And, oh King, when the music sounded today, these boys, Shadrach, Meshach, and Abednego didn't bow, and the music was louder, and we wanted to make sure we were seeing what we say we saw.'

"The king was like, 'What? you're kidding me, right? I'm the king.' The king looked at Shadrach, Meshach, and Abednego and told them on Friday when the music sounded, each of them had better bow. No exceptions.

"He added, 'If you don't, I will have you thrown in the fire.'

"Shadrach, Meshach, and Abednego acknowledged that they understood, not that they would bow. The king sent them away.

"On Friday, when the music sounded, the guard watched, laser-focused on the boys. Sure enough, everyone in the area hit the dirt, but Shadrach, Meshach, and Abednego did not bow. There they stood among the people in plain view for the guard to see these three Hebrew teenagers still standing. They would not bow."

The preacher stopped to take a sip of water. The congregation sat still, waiting for the next part. Many of them were well familiar with the story, but even so, they were simply mesmerized by the preacher's presence and confidence and the manner in which he told the story.

Ninx and Standford had their eyes glued to the preacher, taking in every word. NaCharles lay soundly asleep in his mother's arms. While the preacher sipped the water, Ninx took that moment to kiss his baby's forehead, thanking him for staying quiet all this time. NaCharles squirmed at the touch of his father's warm, loving lips and smiled in his sleep.

The preacher continued. "Shadrach, Meshach, and Abednego were bought before the king again.

"'Why didn't you bow? I thought we came to an understanding?' The king looked at each of them.

"'God is our true God,' said Shadrach.

"'We did understand you, King,' added Meshach.

"'We left saying that we understood your command. We did not say that we would bow, King,' Abednego closed out."

Ninx took the time to read the rest of the scriptures. He wasn't as familiar with the story. He wanted to know what happened to Shadrach, Meshach, and Abednego. He glanced over to Standford, whose eyes were still glued to the preacher, NaCharles was still sleeping peacefully. "You're a good son," he whispered and continued reading. At the end of the chapter, Ninx returned his attention to hear the preacher say, "Know the power of God and trust Him at His Word."

"I will," Ninx whispered. "I will."

He hadn't noticed that he stood in front of the home they had shared for many years. His chest burned with thoughts more than fatigue from his run. He couldn't decide whether to see if Standford was home or make a slow run back to his apartment. He stretched on the sidewalk, trying to sort through the thoughts that consumed him during the run. He had to trust God no matter what, even if it meant he'd have to walk through fire. Shadrach, Meshach, and Abednego survived fire because they trusted in God. They had the faith that God could do the impossible. He needed that kind of faith. "Well, I guess I could start today." He finished stretching and walked up the steps of his previous home. He tapped on the screen and waited.

"Know the power of God and trust Him at His Word."

The sound of footsteps made Ninx stop breathing.

The door opened to a beautiful woman dressed in a floral print dress who looked like she'd been crying a lot.

They hugged and said no words.

CHAPTER 4

What's Your Story?

*H*ave *you read the story of Me-phib'o-sheth? It is the story of grace. The grace that God extends is a precious amount of weight. Think about the weight of grace. His grace is sufficient for thee. She couldn't bring herself to make another visit. It was too hard, as he was her only child. Yet, she dressed slowly to be ready when the doorbell rang. God is merciful and . . .*

Standford looked at her floral print dress and didn't feel as pretty as the dress looked on her. She pranced about the kitchen, trying to recall where she had failed as a parent. She and Ninx had had a good conversation today. He left to run back to his apartment with a renewed spirit. He'd realized, when he arrived on the doorsteps of his former home the other day, that their only child had been in prison for almost three years. Each year was harder than the last.

As he placed his running shoes back in their corner, he also realized that, in all that time, they hadn't talked about or agreed on how their living situation could, should, or would change but, they also didn't disagree on pulling together to support NaCharles. The very first day Ninx arrived on the doorsteps was a silent agreement that they had to come together to support NaCharles and each other. They both had things to consider and plans to act upon at the right time. Ninx retold the story from the tall preacher. He was happy Standford remembered too. "NaCh stayed asleep for the entire sermon." Her smile warmed his heart. He gently touched her face wanting to ask her what happened to them but decided that wasn't the right moment.

She went full circle to come back to the table to stare at the well-prepared breakfast for her and Ninx. She didn't tell him she'd made it for them both because when he showed up at her door, she panicked and just stayed at the door hugging, having a small conversation about past times, when they would visit, and he then headed back to his apartment. *Maybe next time,* she told herself.

The last steam from the eggs and French toast disappeared in the air. The ice in the orange juice had started its slow melt. She promised herself that she wouldn't cry while thinking about the start of NaCharles' third year in prison. She had already taken the two-hour drive with Ninx six times in this new year. Each time was harder than the last. Standford looked at the flowers on the pretty dress and remembered that it was already June. She took another round the kitchen and stared at the near-perfect breakfast. She stared at the eggs, bacon, French toast, and hash browns. Ninx loved hash browns for breakfast. She loved to prepare them for him. She looked at the breakfast as events in her life on a plate that had somehow gone cold. She poked at the eggs and toast, and to her surprise, they were still warm.

"I've been walking around the house for thirty minutes and the breakfast is still rather warm. How is that?"

"Me-phib'o-sheth was shown mercy by David as a promise to his father. Me-phib'o-sheth was a crippled child, lame in both feet. He wasn't allowed to eat at the table because of his appearance; it was perceived as an embarrassment to the family. But David promised to make sure that Me-phib'o-sheth had the best in life and a better life. Do you know the story?"

There was silence in the congregation. Standford looked at Ninx, who shrugged his shoulders at her.

NaCharles yanked his dad's sleeve to say, "I don't know the story either Dad."

"Well, I guess we're about to hear it or we'll have to read it for ourselves." Ninx smiled down at NaCharles. His eyes were innocent and full of curiosity. Ninx loved being a dad. He pulled open his Bible and searched for the story.

Standford whispered, "Honey, he hasn't said the scripture yet, unless you already know where it is."

Ninx smiled at Standford, and she returned a bigger one while directing his attention to the preacher.

At that moment, the preacher said, "For those who are not familiar, please turn with me to II Samuel 9:1–13. I'll read aloud, and I want you to follow along, especially those who are hearing this for the first time or may have heard about it and forgotten."

Ninx looked at Standford and spoke into NaCharles' ear, "Now we won't have to read it later. We better pay attention before Mom gets us." They all laughed a low hearty laugh, and the preacher began to read. His voice was heavy—so much so that he had to loosen his collar as he spoke. One could see the sweat stain on the collar of his orange dress shirt. He wore a dark-green suit, which was a different look, with a beige tie that added attention to the entire outfit, especially the orange dress shirt. He wiped the sweat from his forehead with an orange handkerchief.

"And David said, 'Are there any left in the house of Saul that I might shew him kindness? Jonathan has a son which is lame in both feet. Where is he?' King David sent for him. He came and fell at the king's feet. And David said, 'Fear not, for I will surely shew thee kindness . . . thou shalt eat bread at my table continually.' From that day, Me-phib'o-sheth dwelt in Jerusalem . . . for he did eat continually at the king's table . . . lame in both feet." The preacher paused with his face still in his Bible. Without looking up, he softly asked, "So what's your story?"

Standford tried to wipe some of the tears that flowed down her thin face. She pressed on the floral dress and landed in one of the kitchen chairs. She spoke into the air of the room, meaning for the words to reach God. She returned her thoughts to the preacher in the dark-green suit. The sweat poured from his face. He wiped it with the orange handkerchief and continued.

"My story is grace. David and Jonathan were really good friends. David promised Jonathan that he would see after his family. David gave up something and worked to bestow grace upon Me-phib'o-sheth. When Me-phib'o-sheth sat at the table of King David, no one knew he was lame in both feet."

Just as Christ knows that I'm truly hurt that my only child is in prison for seven years. But only God knows, and He will restore me, and I will know.

"The grace that God extends carries a weight."

That sermon was a long time ago, and today it registered. Standford ate the breakfast she had prepared and waited for Ninx. They would take the long drive to see their only child. Today was a new day to discover God's Word and learn to trust and love Him and take Him at His Word.

The doorbell rang fifteen minutes later. Standford went to the door with a renewed spirit, knowing her story and understanding her situation. She wanted a winning spirit. She pressed the flowers on her dress and opened the door to see her handsome husband—ex-husband—standing there, radiating confidence and hardened trust in God.

"What's our story?" she asked him on the way to the car.

"What do you mean?" Ninx replied as he held the car door open for her.

"You remember the story about King David and Me-phib'o-sheth? Remember the preacher had an orange handkerchief and a bright orange dress shirt with that dark green suit?" They both laughed.

"That was a long time ago, Stan. You still remember that?" He glanced over as he started the car. He was glad that she was able to laugh, even if only briefly.

"That suit was crazy green," he added in an attempt to get her to laugh more. She did just that—heartily—as she buckled her seat beat. She tapped him slightly on his leg as she finished her laugh and turned on the radio. Ninx thought about all the years they'd been married—all the years they'd been divorced. Why had it come to this?

"And that orange handkerchief was *loud*." She laughed some more. After finding a good station, she turned to him and asked again, "As I asked before, Ninx, what's our story?"

"Let me see if I remember right . . ." He was careful not to make another joke. She was serious.

"The story of Me-phib'o-sheth was about King David trying to make amends for a situation gone awry. Are you asking if or how that relates to us?" He paused, careful in choosing his words. Evidently, Standford could see it in his expression.

"Go ahead and say it, Ninx. We're adults." She tapped him lightly on his leg again, which sent sparks up his back, but he knew it was only a cue for him to continue.

"As that relates to us. We had a good marriage as far as I'm concerned. I could've done some things better, and I regret that. Now we have our son who's serving time and we have to make amends so that we can be there for him. It's a shameful situation like Me-phib'o-sheth and his lameness but it's a necessary action on our part like it was for King David for his best friend."

Before Standford could speak, Ninx added, "Stan, we're best friends and parents and we need to be both for NaCharles' sake. We'll need to put aside our differences, whatever those might be, and concentrate so that we can all get through this. That's our story for right now."

The silence in the car was sliced by Standford's response, "Ninx, that's our story. I agree that we could've done a much better job with our marriage, and we should've worked even harder when NaCh first started getting into trouble at school. I own that mistake. We have to do better for NaCh. We can do it. I need to lean on you for strength sometimes if that's all right by you."

"I also own that I should've worked harder when NaCh was falling off. I so much own that."

Standford could feel and see the pain of his failure.

He took her hand and said, "By all means, you know that you can lean on me. Anytime."

They rode the rest of the way to the prison in silence. The music from the radio-filled vehicle. They each sent a silent prayer to heaven, each asking for God to give them the strength and ability to be as King David was to his friend's son, Me-phib'o-sheth, who was lame. No one knew, as he was seated at the table in such a way that no one could detect. NaCharles was serving seven years in prison, and no one really knew. Standford had served time as a young adult, and no one had really known about that either. It *was* known that someone cared for them and helped them through the ordeal with dignity. They prayed to be able to understand their story and be able to tell their story with dignity.

Seven years was a long time, and they both needed strength.

CHAPTER 5

Establishing the Lines of Effort

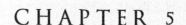

On the drive to the prison, Standford was able to smile in her heart. She took Ninx's hand and wanted badly to ask him why they had allowed their marriage to crumble before their eyes. He was intent on getting to the prison. Every visit, he maintained a positive outlook. NaCharles listened. Ninx sounded like he was giving instructions for NaCharles to mentally survive. Teachable moments. He needed survival tools.

The prison doors were loud and old. Too loud for the space Ninx and Standford occupied themselves while waiting to be screened. Standford always wondered why she'd picked Wednesday to visit. While she did the brief wait today, she realized that exactly four guests showed up on Wednesdays and that the guard population was like three to one per guest in the holding room. Hard to smuggle in illegal goods on Wednesdays. The prison doors' alarm went off again, too loud and old, signaling for them to step into the area to meet their respective prisoner.

NaCharles looked smaller than she remembered from their last visit, but he did have a smile on his face. Standford smiled back. They did their traditional air hug and sat at the small metal table. Ninx always had a story to break the tension in the room. After a while, they automatically looked at him, waiting for him to begin.

"Are you teachable, NaCh?"

NaCharles and Standford looked at each other and then at Ninx. They both wore a "where is this coming from?" expression. Her floral print dress looked out of place in the dim visiting area. There were no pictures on the walls; the shades were drawn, and she noticed that she was the only woman present today. She reverted her attention to hear Ninx laugh his hearty laugh, covering his perfect teeth with one hand.

"I decided to attend Bible school last week and couldn't wait to get here to share the lesson with you today. The topic was "Are You Teachable?" It comes from Ephesians 6:1–4. Children obey your parents in the Lord, for this is right."

Ninx paused to read NaCharles' expression. He had practiced saying this all week and wanted NaCharles to accept it for its meaning, not to put any blame on him. He reached for NaCharles' hand, the guard stepped forward and Ninx let it go. "Just hear me out, Son."

"Dad, I understand. I should've obeyed you both a long time ago, and I realize that. You probably heard that topic at church last week to be able to tell me what it means exactly. Like when we were both sitting at church, trying to understand the story of the guy with the two lame feet." NaCharles smiled to himself for remembering, and Ninx loved him for it. Standford laughed out loud at the "two lame feet" and the bright orange dress shirt. Ninx and NaCharles were glad to hear her laugh. This whole ordeal was trying, and they both knew they had some blame.

NaCharles continued, "Dad, I love you, and no I'm not offended." He looked at his mother and said, "Please continue. Mom may not know this story." Standford made a face as if to say, "Yes I do." They all laughed, and it felt good.

Ninx closed his mind to the prison surroundings to recall the topic last Thursday. He wanted to relive the experience with his wife and son. He told NaCharles about having a teachable spirit. Standford listened intensely.

"The speaker for that night had us read Ephesians chapter 6 verses 1-13. If I was able, I would've bought my Bible with me but I wasn't sure if they'd allow it and if I had would they keep it. I'll ask on the way out. Anyway. The topic was "Are You Teachable?" We're to have a teachable spirit so that we can discover God's Word. Ephesians chapter six is about obeying parents. It says 'Children obey your parents in the Lord, for this is right.' It's just as much for the parent as it is for the child. The speaker said that we must be teachable in order to be good leaders, hence good parents, spouses, employees, friends, children, and so on. We're all to have a teachable spirit." Ninx looked at the time and at his family. They both were all ears as he explained being teachable. He wanted badly to get all the points before their visiting time ran out.

One of the guards had stepped closer to hear Ninx's conversation. Standford noticed that the door guard had also eased closer to them as if they were about to commit a crime inside the prison. The guard nodded toward Standford, gesturing that all was fine. Keeping her eyes on the guard, she touched Ninx lightly on his arm to tell him to continue.

"The speaker stated that we must be willing to listen when God speaks so that we can learn. Don't celebrate what you've done in the past but get ready to move forward in your future. Like Jonah. He didn't do as instructed. He didn't obey. I asked and told you many times during your young life to do this and that. Sometimes you did, and other times you didn't. But I still loved you. I still love you. Jonah was told by God to go and tell of His Word to the people. Jonah didn't, and God punished him for it. But Jonah was teachable. He spent three days in the belly of the fish, learning what God wanted him to do. At the end of the third day, the fish spat Jonah onto the shore, and he went about the business of the Lord. He was given a second chance to do as God instructed."

By this time the door guard was only a few feet away from the three of them, he tried to look elsewhere, appearing busy, but his mind was on the story. With a light chuckle, Ninx continued and made no eye contact with the guard, who had nearly joined the group.

"Jonah was given instructions that he didn't want to follow. He hindered others from hearing the Word of the Lord. Yet, he was given a second chance to get right with God. Before he was released from the fish, he was given the same instructions once more and he went on and did them. He was teachable. Son, we know that you did what you did at the time because that was your best option. That was the decision you made in the moment for whatever reason. God understands that too. Now He's giving you time to think about your second chance. The only thing is that yours is seven years long and not three days. Yours is in a prison and not the belly of a fish. At least that's what I think. That's my only conclusion, and my consolation to you is to keep your spirit in the game and trust in God. Perhaps you need more time than Jonah did to prepare to execute God's instructions. Hence, your second chance. Ask yourself, "Am I teachable?" We don't know. Only you can answer that. What we do know is that you too have a story, as do we, and we think you are teachable and we're teachable too."

He looked at Standford for approval. He could see the tears welling up in her eyes, ready to flow down her face. He looked at NaCharles, who wanted to cry but dared not in front of the guard who was now practically in their conversation. Although there were no other inmates who had visitors, Ninx understood.

When the guard realized that the story ended and he had quickly wiped the few tears from his own face, he motioned for Ninx and Standford to close out. Ninx turned to see that the guest area was empty except for the guard, Ninx, Standford, and NaCharles.

"This needed to be told," Ninx said as he gathered up his small family. "And God has allowed it." Ninx gave the guard a non-verbal thank you at which the guard nodded. Ninx and the guard looked around to make sure there were no others present, and then they launched into a long, much-needed family hug and quickly left the prison visiting area. This time, the gates didn't sound so loud. Walking to the car, Ninx whispered, "God is better than amazing," and within the prison, behind bars, NaCharles felt the same.

The walk to the car this time was filled with hope, faith, grace, and mercy. Ninx, overcome by emotions and beauty, pulled Standford to him and kissed her long and hard.

Standford stepped back to look into his eyes as he asked, "We're good parents and we have a teachable spirit. I've been meaning to ask you, why did we separate and then divorce and how was that good for our son?"

Ninx didn't wait for an answer. He gently slid Standford into the passenger seat and closed the door.

The next four years would be crucial.

Outside of their minds, the drive was long and quiet. Their minds were running a marathon. Each meditated upon the story he told at the prison, and each tried to decide how they could change to be there for their son.

NaCharles was sure to wipe all of his tears and put on his game face before returning to his prison cell. They were mixed tears of joy, relief, and sadness. Yet no tears, regardless of their category, would go over well in the prison atmosphere. He had to present a tough front to survive.

He had served almost three years. Each year, he realized that he really loved and missed his parents and knew that it took for him to be confined to understand and know the will of God in his life. Although he had been practicing the "tough guy" persona, he had yet to use it. And for that, he was truly grateful. He had a massive size cellmate who had yet to give him any trouble. God had looked after Jonah in the fish for three days. He had looked out for NaCharles for three years. He just knew that someone—anyone—would confront him to do a deed in exchange for protection. He almost let the last of his tearful emotions flow but quickly decided against it as he stepped into his cell. He hopped on his top bunk and noticed that his massive cellmate wasn't on the bottom bunk. He was alone for the moment and let the tears flow freely.

He loved his parents, and he loved the life that he had with them. He struggled to agree with himself that he also loved his life with Masha for the good times for whatever they were now worth. He went back to the times his mother had told him that she wasn't a good kid and wanted to do everything she could to make sure her child did none of the bad things she'd done. Disappointingly enough, NaCharles had done all those things and more. He was in prison for seven years. Year one dragged on and he missed his freedom. Year two, he found himself trying to do better mentally, finding some understanding. But that's what prison is about: understanding that freedom, no matter how paltry, is freedom. At the start of year three, he concluded that this was his fate to prepare for his second chance. His Dad had said that God is a God of second chances.

He cried into his pillow and remembered the song "Yes."

His mind drifted to a happy time in his life when . . .

NaCharles had convinced his parents that he was old enough or at least mature enough to sit by himself. Standford laughed. Ninx gave him a stern fatherly look. NaCharles knew that his father was serious about God—not necessarily church facilities but God. And since God was a big part of church, then that was equally important.

"I will, Dad. I'll listen and be able to tell you the sermon at any time, whenever you ask."

NaCharles watched the angelic figure with full attention. Ninx motioned for NaCharles to take a seat of his choice and turned to guide his wife to another section of the church to allow NaCharles full range to exercise his maturity. To his surprise, NaCharles decided to sit closer to the front for he had seen a girl dressed like an angel that caught his attention.

The Praise Dance Ministry was up next. One of the members took the stage and gave a thumbs up to the audio crew. The music began immediately. The angelic figure he'd seen earlier moved with the music. Her arms were graceful, giving a message of hope and change. NaCharles listened to the words as he watched the angelic figure move on the stage. The words of the song were belted across the church. *"My heart and soul say yes. If I told you what's required of me, would your heart and soul say yes?"*

NaCharles thought this was one of his better Sundays. He was forced to come with his parents, but the angelic figure on the stage was so beautiful that he was actually glad he came. Her bronze skin lit the stage. The dress flowed evenly with each movement. Her hair was pulled into a long ponytail and matched her movements. She wore white gloves and little white dance shoes. NaCharles thought he could smell her light fragrance as she twirled on the stage. When the song ended, he made up in his mind to pay attention to the sermon as he watched the angelic figure take a seat two rows in front of him. He also promised his dad that he'd be able to retell the sermon when prompted. As the angelic figure took her seat, he could actually smell her light perfume and took another moment to repeat her movements in his mind, singing the words of the song: *"My heart and soul says yes. If I told you what's required of me, would your heart and soul say yes?"*

The administrative clerk took the podium. Her blue puffy sleeves seemed to cover her face, and her voice was serious. The church was extra quiet as she belted out all the events for the month. She finished reading the announcements and walked gracefully back to her seat. NaCharles made a note to attend Praise Dance practice on Tuesday at 7 p.m. He could get a better look at the angelic figure. He also could learn a thing or two. He moved to the offering tray just a little slower today and put in the two dollars his mother had given him. He was doing as instructed, and he liked the way it made him feel. He smiled at the young praise dancer. She returned a half-smile. "She's still cute with that funky attitude," he said under his breath. He dropped the two dollars in the tray and took in the long hug from one of the church mothers. At least she was excited about his genuine gesture. He walked back to his seat and readied himself for the sermon, which he intended to listen to and take to heart. He peered up the two rows to see the angelic figure who appeared to be totally attentive to the actions in the pulpit.

The pastor stepped up to the pulpit, wearing a black robe with a red cross on either side of the gold breast-plate-like front. The sleeves were trimmed in a thick red zig-zag patterned thread that was easily seen by those sitting in the last pew. NaCharles traced them with his mind and wondered why the pastor wore this particular robe today. The pastor placed his hands on the sides of the podium, and NaCharles was able to see the gold Rolex on his right wrist and the 24k tennis bracelet on his left wrist. He also noticed that his hands were pretty big for his size. At first, he thought about how much his outfit was worth; then, he remembered he'd always been told that just because a pastor dresses well and owns a nice car doesn't mean he's taking money from the church. NaCharles decided that the pastor was a good person with great taste in clothes and accessories with enough money of his own to pay for them.

When the pastor spoke, his voice was as gentle as the fine robe and accessories, "Blind. But now I see. Today's sermon will come from St. John 9:1–7. Go with me to the scriptures, and let's read them together. It's only seven verses."

His large hands turned the pages of his Bible, which appeared to be too small for him. NaCharles was lost in thought about the pastor and the angelic figure in front of him. He took a short pause to observe and approximate the congregation. He looked at his parents and found that they were engaged in the reading. He didn't own a Bible but promised to be able to relay the story if or when his dad asked. Suddenly, on second thought, he panicked and looked about the church, searching for a Bible. He knew that most churches had extra Bibles for visitors. He looked to the usher closest to him. She evidently read his mind because she handed him a Bible already turned to the scripture. He gave her a warm smile of relief and started to read the verses.

NaCharles mouthed the words coming from the Bible. "Who did this sin? . . . Neither hath sinned . . . I must work the works . . . I am the light of the world . . . and he anointed the blind man's eyes and told him to go wash, which he did . . . and came back seeing." He paused and looked around to see if he'd missed the pastor's interpretation. "Now that's a miracle that I can retell when asked." NaCharles laid the borrowed Bible on his lap and gave his attention to the pastor, mentally tracing the thick red zig-zag pattern. The usher, who had given him the Bible, noticed his attentiveness and smiled in his direction. He kept his eyes on the pastor, making the usher even more pleased at his attentiveness.

"Have you ever had something happen in your life and you thought it was unfair? Take the blind man who was born blind, not because of the sins of his father or his father's father. Things just happened. It wasn't a punishment. Think about that for a minute." The pastor looked about the congregation. His eyes landed on NaCharles, who continued to pay close attention. He thought of a lot of things in life that were unfair, but he wasn't blind. The pastor stayed on NaCharles for a moment longer and shifted his gaze across the general congregation.

He continued. "St. John chapter nine verses one through seven talks about a young man who was born blind, and Jesus restored his eyesight. A topic I can use today is "Blind but, Now I See." Jesus already knew His purpose. When His disciples saw the blind man, they immediately asked, 'Who sinned?'

"'No one,' Jesus replied.'

"'He is in such a state to allow me to work a miracle in his life to show the world that God is able to do all things—even the impossible." The pastor's voice remained soft as if speaking to a small child. NaCharles smiled because he knew he'd be able to remember the story of the blind man and Jesus' miracle of sight. The pastor continued to talk about being physically and spiritually blind. Jesus used the blind man's circumstance to validate His presence. To show all present that He could do the impossible.

The blind man was able to see after being blind his entire life. Jesus made it possible. Never did it state that the blind man complained of his situation. No one committed a sin to cause his blindness. Yet, God in all His glory, blessed the blind man and gave him physical and spiritual sight. The pastor stepped out of the pulpit. He raised his Rolex arm and it slid into the sleeve of the robe. The two crosses seemed larger as the pastor moved to stand at the front of the pulpit. NaCharles continued to pay attention. *Why did Jesus heal the blind man? Why is the pastor speaking about physical and spiritual blindness?*

"Allow God to use your circumstances to validate your blessings. At times, you may think that all is against you, but God has a plan for your life. Some of us are blind, and we want to see. Some of us are blind and don't want to see. Some of us have been handed an "unfair" advantage in life, and we want to be redeemed. And all of us need Jesus to be the Miracle Maker. So, go about your life doing the right thing and no matter the circumstances, trusting and believing in God will allow Him to use your circumstances to validate His greatness. Trusting in God will allow you to see."

The pastor returned to the pulpit. As he stood at the pulpit, he surveyed the congregation, making sure that his words were understood. He was handed a glass of orange juice with ice that clattered as he gulped down half of the contents. NaCharles quickly read the verses again, as he had to be ready for when (not if) his dad asked him to tell the story.

"God will give you a new beginning as He did with the blind man." The pastor took his seat, and the minister seated to his right rose to the podium. The usher came to retrieve the Bible from NaCharles and told him that he was a good boy, well-behaved, and that his parents should be proud to have such a son. He smiled in the usher's direction as she quickly replaced the Bible and returned to her post. He then returned his attention to the pulpit.

NaCharles lay in the too-small, too-hard prison bed tears still streaming. He was as the blind man, and he needed God to give him a new beginning and use his current circumstance to validate His power. In moments, as if on cue, NaCharles stopped crying and realized that he could have a new beginning. He rose up on his elbows, thinking. He recalled how many times his father asked him to tell the story of the blind man every time he got into a situation that he thought wasn't fair. He had to tell the story every time he made an unwise decision. He would tell the story of the blind man, feel better, and go about his day with a renewed spirit. Sometimes, he would tell the story just to get the conversation over, and other times, he would tell the story with genuine zest. As a youngster, he still made unwise decisions and still felt like some things weren't fair, but that was a long time ago. Maybe God had forgotten about him since he'd gone so far off the path of doing right. Or maybe he'd forgotten that he needed God. He lay back down on the prison bed and let the tears return. He thought about his parents, their separation, their divorce, the time in court, Masha and her freedom and empty promises, and he thought again of the blind man. He recalled that the pastor had said that the blind man was physically blind while others were spiritually blind.

NaCharles prayed through his tears. "Lord, I can't see where this is going. I couldn't see where I was going. I'm not asking you to take away the punishment that I rightfully earned. I'm asking that you help me to serve my time and learn from it to help others. I learned from church not to make promises to You that I know I probably won't keep, so I'll just ask that You protect me in here, keep my parents safe, and give me a new beginning. A beginning that I can later put to good use. Lord, please forgive me. Help me through the trials that I'm currently going through. Please help me to be triumphant in the end. I want to learn of You and use my time wisely. Not to get in more trouble in here and later get out and be a prison preacher. I want to really serve You on the other side of these bars and prison walls. I want to go from trials to triumphs. I need a new beginning. Amen."

CHAPTER 6

A New Beginning

Watch and pray that you may not fall into temptation, for it will come and tempt you. He looked about the cell and suddenly felt that it was all just a little bit more bearable. He felt in the darkness for the small Bible he had borrowed from the prison library. He was happy that he'd learned to read. He couldn't quite understand the words, but he could at least read them. "The spirit is willing but the flesh is weak . . ."

It was his father's birthday. For years, he remembered, he and his mom would bake a cake and put three candles on it regardless of his father's age. He loved helping his mother put the ingredients in the large mixing bowl. Even after he'd reached his early teenage years, he still enjoyed the time making the cake. First, she would stir the mix with a large spoon by hand, and then she would use the electric mixer. The cake was usually a different flavor, and there was different frosting each time. NaCharles had abandoned the cake-baking tradition when he went way off the radar of righteousness. He missed all of his father's birthdays after he'd turned fifteen. He didn't even think about it until now.

One particular year, NaCharles asked his mother, "Why do we only use three candles instead of Dad's real age? Why do you insist on baking a different kind of cake with a different frosting each year?" His mother told him that each year was a new beginning and the three candles represented more patience and more wisdom and more understanding. NaCharles didn't quite understand. He resolved that since it made his mom happy, he was as well—and his dad was certainly.

He looked about the small prison cell, which seemed to feel a little different, not as dull and heart-wrenching. NaCharles could feel a little hope building up in his soul. He tried to smile despite his tears. He decided to treat each year of his sentence like his father's birthday cake; he would strive for something spiritually different in the next four more years. This would be his new beginning. It would be something for him to strive for and look forward to. It would be something to keep his mind occupied. He wiped his tears and tried to get some rest. A dream came immediately. Or was it a memory from his childhood? Whatever the case, it gave him a little peace of mind.

"Matthew 26:36–45 talks about being spiritually asleep. Let's take a moment to read the verses," said the preacher and started to read aloud. ". . . Sit ye here while I go yonder to pray . . . Lord let this cup pass . . . if it be thy will . . . He returned to find the disciples asleep . . . He asked, ye could not stay awake for one hour? He went again to pray and returned to find them yet asleep . . . A third time, and the disciples still slept . . . Wake now; we must go." The preacher closed his Bible and stood silently. NaCharles had never seen a preacher close his Bible. *This must be a serious sermon*, he thought. He matched the preacher's silence and waited. The preacher wore a white robe with gold trim on the sleeves and collar. His cream-color skin made him look like an angel sent straight from heaven to give the Word of the Lord for today. When he showed his very white teeth, it was like his whole face disappeared. Everything was white as fresh-fallen snow. The only exception was the gold trimming on the sleeves and the collar. NaCharles continued to wait out the silence. It finally broke when the preacher spoke, showing all that white.

"Saints, Jesus Christ wants us to stay awake; watch and pray that we may not fall into temptation. The spirit is willing, but the flesh is weak. We are spiritually asleep—or nodding off. Jesus prayed a hard prayer. He wanted to get out of the deed that He had to do so we all could be here today under the sound of my voice." He silenced again and looked about the congregation. This was the opportunity for everyone to think about what he had just said. *We are asleep, oblivious to what God wants us to do. We're either lazy or lack the strength to keep our eyes open and do the will of the Lord.*

The church was so quiet, everyone could practically hear one another breathing. NaCharles tried not to look directly at the preacher with all that white. He thought his mind was playing tricks on him as he really thought he saw wings coming from behind the preacher each time he showed his teeth making everything go white. He shivered a bit but continued to listen to the silence. He could hear himself breathing unevenly adding to the mixtures of the congregation. The preacher closed off his white teeth and the wings seemed to disappear immediately. He then walked a few steps in front of the podium and quickly returned to his Bible as if he had just remembered what he wanted to say.

"You have to accept what God wants of you even if *you* don't want it. Jesus didn't want to die for the sins of the world, but He had to do it. He did do it. Thank God. We don't want to go through the trials and tribulations that come with living for Christ, but we have to in order to be triumphant in the end. I hope you understand. At times, we find ourselves in the worst situations; we fall asleep. We are willing to do what the Lord requires, but at times, we fall asleep; our eyes get heavy with spiritual fatigue. Then, we think we can't get it done."

NaCharles continued to listen as the sermon progressed.

"But God will never leave you nor forsake you. Even when you fall asleep, He will still take you and pull you up. He will wake you as He did to disciples."

"He loves you," NaCharles added as he came back to the realness of prison. He could feel the dry tears on both cheeks. He knew he had to wake from his spiritual slumber and move forward under the promises of God. He wanted to surprise his parents with his renewed strength. He could go from trials to triumphs. He believed it for the moment and prayed to have it manifested in his prison life, so he'd be prepared for his walk with Christ outside of prison.

He remembered his dad's birthday was fast approaching. It would be the first time in a long time that he actually cared, and he wouldn't be able to see the cake and candles. Although he hadn't spent a lot of time with his parents after meeting Masha, he knew his mom continued the tradition. Or maybe not since they divorced. They seemed so good together. He wondered why they really separated and subsequently divorced. He wished he could bake that cake, with a mystery icing and three candles. He too needed a new beginning. "Lord, please help me to make it. The only way I'm going to make it is if you allow it. Bake me a cake with icing and three candles—wisdom, patience, and understanding. I need You. I have such a long way to go. I fell asleep for a long time. Now I think I'm awake—blind but awake—and I think I'm ready to change for the better."

"Lights out, mates!"

NaCharles jumped at the sound with excitement in his heart. Tomorrow would be the first day of his new beginning. He lay still and prayed again, asking God for the strength he would need to move forward. The darkness hid his tears as they began a slow, quiet flow down his cheeks and into the poorly-filled pillow.

CHAPTER 7

Stay in the Fight

H e decided to take up boxing to help pass the time. Not so much to defend himself but more so to practice stamina and discipline. His first workout proved to him that three minutes in the ring was a long time. And holding his fists in the guarded position was a lot harder than he thought. He'd seen a lot of boxing on television but hadn't thought about the strength and stamina it takes to stay in the fight for three minutes.

NaCharles wasn't sure if he'd ever have to fight for his life. Year four ended with his new beginning still intact. As painful as it was, he took his mind back five years to the time he committed the crime with Masha. He hadn't thought about the crime, but he knew he needed to in order to better move forward. His heart burned, and tears began to well up in his eyes as he pictured in his mind's eye the young man sprawled on the ground after having run out of the apartment. He had to admit to the insidious nature of his crime. He had to revisit the crime in order to have closure and really begin his new beginning. The man, whose name he didn't know, probably wouldn't get that chance. The trial was so quick. He strained to remember if the man had died right after the trial or there had been a possibility he might still recover. He promised he wouldn't give the authorities Masha's name. He loved her too much. Today, he felt as though she didn't love him as she'd said because she hadn't come to visit him in five years! His only visitors were his parents. No one else. He felt for the man he'd hurt. He probably had a family and friends that loved him.

The courtroom was full of people who loved the hurt man. NaCharles strained to remember the man's name. That wasn't important to his new beginning either. He would need to pray for the man by name. He forced his tears to stop for his situation and concentrated on the details of the trial. His mind went straight to the good-looking female judge. He remembered how he thought his own good looks would land him a lighter sentence. *"This isn't about me or the judge. It's about Steven Mulberry."* The name coming from his mouth startled him. He looked about the cell as if he'd committed another crime. His heart leaped in his chest. He remembered! He remembered Steven Mulberry. Steven Ralph Mulberry, to be exact. He began to pray for forgiveness, asking God to please deliver Steven Ralph Mulberry to safety. Not asking for a reduction of his sentence but to have mercy on the innocent man he'd hurt or killed. He then asked for mercy on his own life as he served his seven-year sentence. He prayed for strength to stay in the "fight".

"II Timothy the second chapter, and we'll begin at the third verse. It reads, 'Endure hardness as a good soldier of Jesus Christ . . . If we suffer, we shall reign with him. Study to shew thyself approved." The preacher stopped reading while the congregation struggled to understand the meaning. Trying to follow his logic, NaCharles stirred in his seat as did the three older ladies seated next to him. The medium-sized church smelled like fresh flowers. The extra clean windows made the colored designs brighten up the entire church. He tried to look as if he understood. He really didn't. The lady nearest him touched his arm and whispered, "Don't feel bad, we feel the same." She offered a forced smile, and he returned a genuine one. He decided to wait it out.

The preacher continued. "II Timothy—the first chapter is about courage and stamina, to those of you who have a confused look on your face."

Laughter filled the church, matching the brightness. The members evidently trusted the preacher to present the Word of God.

"I've been preaching the Word of God for ten years. For much of that time, I lacked the stamina needed to stay in the fight. I was like those disciples. I too had fallen into a spiritual sleep. I had given up. I had grown tired. The life of a preacher is exhausting. Sometimes I still feel fatigued . . . and hopeless, ready to give up. Sometimes I need renewed stamina. Living for Christ could be discouraging. It's hard to bring forth the Word of God sometimes. That's why we need to stick to II Timothy, especially the study to shew thyself approved part. Study to be encouraged. Study to increase stamina. Study to be patient. Study to stay in the fight."

The preacher could see the congregation come alive. NaCharles looked down the row to the three ladies seated next to him. They were fully engaged, now nodding in agreement. The lady next to the one who touched his arm leaned forward to smile and nod in his direction. He returned both.

"I had to condition to sustain the three minutes it takes for someone to cause you to doubt God and turn on Him. I had to *know* the word to stay in the fight and gain with winning punches. I had to practice keeping my hands and arms up like I was praising my way out of a compromising situation. It's easy for me to lift my hands to God and bless His name. It's easier now than before. I had to remind myself to be patient with God's people—and that includes the sinners. I had to stand still and know what God can do. I had to watch Him throw those combination punches and follow through with grace and speed. Saints, I encourage you to be strong in the grace . . . be able to teach others . . . and the Lord will give thee understanding in all things . . . for if we suffer, we shall reign . . . put them in remembrance . . . Study to shew thyself approved . . . rightly dividing the word of truth. Let everyone in the building please stand to your feet."

NaCharles rose to his feet from the kneeling position on the cell floor. He tried to remember how he ended up on his knees in the first place. At the moment, it didn't matter. His mind was clear. He pressed the sides of his prison wear, washed his face in the small basin, and waited for the cell doors to open for the morning activities. He decided he'd go to the boxing sessions and stick to it. Not for prison protection but to begin the regiment of staying in the spiritual fight, which seemed at the moment a lot harder than a physical fight—and certainly longer than three minutes.

He looked around the cell, wondering what happened to his cellmate. When he thought about it, he couldn't recall the last time the big guy was in his cell. He was too afraid to inquire, so he decided to wait a couple more days and then ask.

He stepped into the dimly-lit hallway of the prison, feeling renewed. He looked about for his cellmate, then headed to sign up for boxing lessons. He knew it would include a regiment that his small frame could probably handle. He'd need to bulk up quickly, as his handsome face would eventually attract too many of the wrong kind of men, and serving time of any kind was too long. NaCharles wanted to avoid being "asked out" or forced into a relationship. He was grateful it hadn't happened yet but wanted to be prepared. He hustled to the makeshift gym area. To his surprise, there weren't a lot of guys there. The ones that had shown were about his size, and they were as handsome as he, also wanting to make sure they weren't taken advantage of so early in their sentence.

"Okay, ladies. Go get a pair of boxing gloves and the rest of the accessories, and let's see what you already got. By the looks of this morning's crowd, you're the pretty girls of the flock. Feast or famine. Predator or prey. I got it. I have one more year and an old lady waiting, so don't worry about me hitting on any of you good-looking gals. Plus, my old lady's a real woman and she looks a lot better than all of you." He laughed and the small group of good lookers laughed uncomfortably. NaCharles knew he was right. His purpose was two-fold; stay in the fight and protect himself. He went to find a set of gloves to fit his small manly hands.

"Get all of the armor," shouted the instructor. You'll need all of the accessories for this session. Trust me. You'll wish you had more after this first bout."

NaCharles slowly and carefully picked his items, thinking back on a sermon he heard and his father constantly reminding him about when he was a young boy.

"Be strong in the Lord and the power of His might. Put on the whole armor of God." The pastor stood at least six feet and some inches in the pulpit. His long robe barely touched the top of his shoes. The congregation was asked to turn to Ephesians 6:10–17. Ninx looked over to NaCharles, nodding to say that he should know these verses. Standford patted him on his hand, and he returned the nod to Ninx.

"Saints, turn with me to the book of Ephesians chapter six, beginning at verse ten." The pastor waited as the pages rustled throughout the church. Ninx and Standford were ready to read. NaCharles was impressed as he looked up the book in the table of contents. Before everyone was on their feet, he finally found it. Although he knew most of it by heart, he still wanted to be sure he was saying the words correctly. He mouthed the words as the pastor said the words out loud, putting emphasis on certain words.

"Finally, my brethren, be strong in the Lord . . . Put on the whole armor . . . that ye may be able to stand . . . for we wrestle against . . . the darkness of the world . . . Wherefore take . . . the whole armor of God . . . which is the Word of God."

The pause was long yet necessary. The congregation remained standing. The pastor stood as well, head to the heavens and arms stretched in no particular direction. NaCharles watched his parents take each other's hands. He smiled again, knowing that he had the best parents in the world and he would do as instructed and take the whole armor of God so that he could fight off the evils of the world.

Standing near the boxing gear, NaCharles was reminded that he had allowed Masha to remove his armor, costing him seven years. He hadn't done as his parents had instructed. Now he grabbed what he considered the best armor and headed to the area with the other soon-to-be boxers.

The inmate instructor told the potential boxer inmates that they would have (or already had) predators lurking around waiting to get them in a compromising situation, and they'd need to defend themselves without committing another crime while locked up. "It happens a lot more than you think," he added.

The good-looking prisoners listened with full attention. A few of them muffled about how they would kill an inmate if he touched him. The instructor let them blow off the steam and stress associated with being the prison prey and then interjected.

"Ladies, listen up please. Don't let the thought of the possibility cause you to lose focus on the purpose. When you do that, you actually hinder your ability to protect yourself in the simplest situations."

NaCharles nearly froze where he stood and recalled a certain preacher . . .

"As Christians, we are like spiritual prey and the spiritual predators will test your faith. That is the reason we must wear the whole armor of God, not some of it. We have to trust in the ability of God, the agility of God, and the stability of God. Don't let the devil hinder your progress toward eternal life. Invest in the gospel gear of God. Get the good stuff. Get that Bible with the extra-large words even if your eyesight is 20/20."

The congregation laughed.

"Let the devil know that you have a heavy sword which is the word of God." The preacher briefly paused, referred to his notes, and continued.

"Ladies, think back on when you got your engagement ring. Some of you got those mile-long ones that you could see from across the street, and others of you got the Cracker Jack size. You know the ones that require glasses or a magnifying glass to see all those tiny fake diamonds. Get that mile-long word and have it with you. Trust that when your armor is on, no harm will come to you. But I caution you, you have to know how to use the armor. It doesn't do much good to have that mile-long diamond on your finger if the marriage is sour. Sometimes, light weight is the best weight for you. Just be sure to have the armor and know how to use it with your unwavering trust in the Word of God. The shield of faith will protect you. Always use it."

NaCharles didn't want to hinder his chances of getting parole at the appointed time, and he definitely didn't want to get in an unnecessary physical confrontation with a would-be attacker or rapist or whatever they were called in this situation. He poised as the instructor introduced day one of his road to becoming a physical fighter. He would read and study the Bible to become a spiritual fighter. "Be strong in the Lord and in the power of His might," he whispered as he executed the punch combinations, one-two, one-two, one-two-three, duck, guard, repeat. Three minutes is a long time for boxing. Seven years is an even longer time to have the potential to be in a three-minute situation. Forever is even a longer time to trust God in all things until He returns.

One-two, one-two, one-two-three, duck, guard repeat. Stamina.

CHAPTER 8

What Is a Christian?

*S*he made up her mind to apologize and ask for a second chance to make things right with her family. She wanted to seek counseling to be sure she'd make a good decision and stick to it. She knew she still loved him and that it wasn't entirely his fault that they had become as they were. She thought herself a Christian. Now she wasn't so sure. What is a Christian, really?

Standford stood in the doorway of the house she'd lived in alone for the past four years. A lot had happened in that time as she tried to recall where the wrong had been done. She forced back unwanted tears. She'd been crying all day and even into the night. She cried about the life she'd lived and the hard time she gave her parents. She cried about the way she let NaCharles stray because she thought Ninx was too hard on him. She cried out of guilt and regret; had she allowed Ninx to raise their son to be a man, he probably wouldn't be in prison serving a seven-year sentence. She cried because she had failed to maintain her marriage and protect her son from the predators of the world. It was her job to not let her only child become prey to the world. She didn't stay in the fight. She didn't wear her armor of God.

"Am I a true Christian?" she said, loudly enough to startle herself in the quiet house. "What is a Christian anyway? Am I a *real* Christian?"

She searched her memory for an answer.

The pastor introduced Minister Greenwell to the congregation. Minister Greenwell stood well over six feet—almost seven feet—from where the congregation sat. Standford found herself stretching her neck to take in his full view. The minister began almost immediately.

"What is a Christian?"

On cue, a member of the congregation shouted out an inaudible response. There were about six mothers from the third pew looking anxiously about the church as if to reprimand the culprit. Standford laughed a low one at the sight of the mothers craning their neck and shifting their eyes, looking toward the sound of the remark.

"That was a rhetorical question," Minister Greenwell replied.

When the congregation settled and the six mothers returned their heads to the front, he continued. "What is a Christian? We may think that a Christian is someone who believes in God. Or perhaps someone who has been baptized. What about a member of a church? My favorite response is a Christian is someone who goes to church. Those are all pretty good answers, but it doesn't define a Christian."

Standford sat looking directly at the minister thinking that those were pretty decent descriptions or definitions. The question remained, though: what was the actual definition? She waited patiently, hoping the minister would clear the air. Instead, he stared out at the congregation as if to gauge their response. The member who had shouted out earlier kept silent. Now was perhaps the time to shout out.

The awkward silence lingered until the minister continued.

"Christ lives in a Christian. Just because someone attends church doesn't make them a Christian. Being baptized doesn't make one a Christian. Being a member of a church with excellent attendance and dutifully dedicated positions doesn't make you a Christian. It just makes you dedicated. And before you think it, no. Believing in God does not make you a Christian. It makes you a believer." He stopped there, knowing he had thoroughly confused the entire congregation. Standford looked puzzled and checked the faces of those she considered devoted Christians. They each had a puzzled look that almost matched hers. She silenced her mind, waiting for the explanation that was sure to come.

"Go to Proverbs 4:23. Keep thy heart . . . out of it are the issues of life. A Christian is one who has a mind through which Christ thinks and acts. A Christian is a voice from which God speaks. Deuteronomy 6:5 says thou shall love the Lord with all thy heart. The voice through which Christ speaks."

The church took to their feet.

Standford let the tears roll. She had her answer. She hadn't allowed Christ to speak. As a matter of fact, she did a great deal of talking and very little listening. She had to redefine her status as a Christian. She needed help so she could help NaCharles. But she needed Ninx to help her to help NaCharles. And she needed God in her life for real to even begin the help process at all. She vowed to dig out her spiritual armor and start wearing it.

The bell rang, and she headed to the door with a new plan in mind. She opened the door to see a smiling Ninx as if he'd read her mind. Through near-perfect teeth, he said, "I've missed you and we need to talk on our way to see NaCh."

He grabbed her hand and led her to the waiting car before she could give a response. They drove in silence to the prison for their Wednesday visit. Standford had somehow forgotten that it was Wednesday—just for a moment. The days and months seemed to all roll together. In the comfortable silence, Standford reflected on how she would take the first move toward allowing God to lead her. She looked out the window, watching the trees and empty field after empty field. She struggled to decide the conversation topic. She understood that her family was just in a bad situation. She'd have to figure out a way to turn the situation into a positive like the rags to riches concept. *Trials to triumphs*, she thought happily. This was a trial from God, testing her faith and trust in His promises. She felt like she was losing but remembered that she had to stay in the fight for the "full round." She smiled out the window as she felt confidence and the promises of God fill her spirit. Yes, she would be triumphant in the midst of her trials. Her next mission was how could she bring Ninx and NaCharles along as well.

The traffic seemed to move in slow motion. A few horns blasted long angry-sounding beeps while others blurted out short anxious sounding honks. Ninx moved with patience and renewed hope. Standford smiled inside with a feeling that they would get through this nightmare together, with the promises of God; triumphant.

The last angry-sounding horn trailed Ninx into the prison parking lot. The weight on his heart as he stood on the porch of the house that he and Standford had once shared lifted away at the same time he placed the car in park. He had pushed aside what he said he'd need to talk with her about. He could feel that she was in deep thought and figured his conversation could wait. Standford could hear him sigh heavily, but she acted as if she hadn't heard nor felt the relief. She would let him take her hand as they walked to the entrance of the prison. She was a Christian, she told herself and vowed to be an even better one from this day forward; she had to be led by the Spirit and truly worship God.

She struggled slightly to begin a conversation. "Ninx, do you ever wonder how we got here and where we're going?" She hoped her voice wasn't cracking. She allowed him to hold her hand as they walked up to the entrance. Ninx took several steps before responding. "We'll talk after this visit. I have a few things on my mind and I also have a funny feeling that we're thinking the same things. I didn't want to interrupt your thoughts in the car. We have to reunite as a family if we're going to get through this with God as the leader." He stopped short of the entrance and looked her in the eyes. She tried not to cry, but the tears were welling up. He placed his hand on her cheeks, catching the first streams of tears. He wiped them quickly and hugged her, whispering in her ear, "We must be led by the Spirit and truly worship God. Can we do that?"

The prison entrance gate opened, allowing the four visitors in for the first search.

"Wednesdays are still the best days to visit. I'm going to let you talk to NaCh today. I've got a feeling that you have a story to share and a plan to move us forward."

They let go of each other's hands as they walked through the gate.

CHAPTER 9

Do as God Commands

H e sat on the steps with the boxing gloves hanging from his knee. He wanted to be good so that he could protect himself. He could hear the instructor repeating, "Do like I tell you, NaCh. Man, you got to do like I tell you." He ignored him every time. He wanted to make the inmates respect him. A first-round knockout would seal his safety. At least that's what he thought. Now here he sat, reviewing all of his mistakes. Do like I tell you. All he had to do was follow the commands from the tower.

The one thing he needed to stand close to God on was handling temptation. Initially, the first deal handed to him he'd take it. After four years behind bars, he wasn't so sure that was his best option. He learned the hard way to take all commands from the tower. The parole board would meet again in a year, and he wanted to be ready to prove that he could do right by his freedom. The boxing match was a bust. He should have handled his frustration with calm. He could hear the inmate boxing coach shouting the commands, but he was so tempted to finish the scrimmage in record time, he folded, ignoring all commands from the tower.

The red boxing gloves concealed the blood stains from the fight. He sat on the stairs, wiping the bloody sweat from his forehead. The boxing scrimmage had turned out to be all that NaCharles thought it wouldn't be. The grand event took place in the open field of the prison yard. The spectators were ushered to the perimeter of the makeshift boxing ring. The shuttle of the inmates started two hours before the scrimmage. Security was increased for the event. NaCharles noticed a few of the late-shift correctional officers were on duty. A guard stood at each corner of the boxing ring, which had been engineered with white sturdy tape and roped off to the weight benches from the common yard. The inmates shouted their favored competing boxer by their nickname; Lil' Biggie, Tak Down, These Fists, and NaCharles had a few shouts of Quiet Storm. His nickname.

The open field was packed with every inmate, and the additional guards were placed strategically about the field. The night before and over the intercom this morning were the event rules as well as the punishment for those who couldn't follow them.

"Quiet Storm" aka NaCharles Mon, inmate number 569324, paced noisily about the field in the area designated for the inmate boxers and their inmate coaches. He uncomfortably did a little jig to get the crowd motivated. He wasn't sure if he promoted his availability to the select or his fighting skills to those who had come to actually watch the event. He continued to pace and showed general gratitude to the multitude of inmates present. NaCharles' prison boxing coach approached him. "Be sure to take all commands from the tower. You'll get frustrated for sure, but listen to the sound of my voice."

The roaring of the inmates almost sounded like a prison riot. The guards stood rigidly at their posts, looking about the crowd for any reason to use the many weapons they toted. NaCharles looked into the crowd at no one in particular and begin his prancing and shadow-boxing warm-ups. He glanced at the temporary clock on the far east wall that had been hung only for the event. Ten minutes to his debut. He reminded himself to take all commands from the tower. He wanted to be mentally prepared to listen and spring to action, unlike . . .

"In chapter five of II Kings is the story of Naaman, who was a leper and wanted to be clean. Healed of his leprosy." The minister allowed the congregation to pick their brain, trying to remember the story. He walked about the pulpit until he figured they'd had enough time to recall. "What can you do for a person of position? The king was intent on standing before Jesus and asking for an extraordinary miracle in his life. A theatrical act of healing. He was simply instructed by the servant of Elisha to go to the Jordan River and wash seven times."

The minister filled the space on the pulpit as he lifted his head, rising to his full seven feet. He appeared as a giant in the small church. His voice vibrated from the pulpit to the back pew. The congregation sat still, listening to the rendition of a familiar Bible story. The minister took the liberty to assume the chuckles meant some were familiar with the story.

"I can see and hear that some of you probably know the story of Naaman. Which also tells me that you know that he was stubborn. Before I go any further, let me give you my title for today." He paused to decide if he should go with his original title or change it; he ultimately stayed with the original. "*Do as God Commands*" and the subtitle is "*Take All Commands from the Tower.*"

Claps and amens filled the small church. The minister plastered a smile, showing his near-perfect teeth with the exception of a small chip on the front right tooth; otherwise, they were perfect.

"When I was in high school, I joined the wrestling team. I wanted to prove to my peers that I could protect myself." Seeing that the congregation gave him a funny look since he now stood at seven feet and was in very good shape, he immediately added. "I didn't always look this good," he added. That statement seemed to have been favored by the young single women, who covered their faces blushing. The mothers appeared to make attempts to hush the growing laughter, and the married women wondered for a second if the minister was still within his biblical rights with such a remark. Smiling at the raucous, he waited for the congregation to settle down. He then continued.

"Now, back to wrestling. I joined the wrestling team to learn some signature moves I could use when Richard, Scottie, and Plus cornered me in the boys' restroom after lunch." Gauging the congregation, he explained. "I'm not sure why they called that boy Plus, and I was in no position to ask. I only knew him as Plus, and to this day, I'm not sure what his real name is."

NaCharles had promised his mother that he would come to church for her one last time before leaving with Masha. Standford had half-hoped that Masha would come with him and she could convince them both that their relationship wasn't a good idea. She still felt in her spirit that Masha was older than the nineteen years she claimed. Standford knew that NaCharles was lovestruck, though, and she didn't want to lose all contact with her only child. NaCharles, on the other hand, took the invitation as an opportunity—a chance to fix their tattered relationship and to show his mother that Masha was a good woman for him.

After thinking it over and talking to Masha, NaCharles came to the small church alone. He had stopped by his father's apartment the day before and he knew Ninx would be soul-deep in church today. It didn't take him long to find his elegant mother sitting in the middle of the small church. She had saved a chair for him and smiled warmly as she patted the seat. She also seemed relieved to see that he had decided to come alone since her time with him had been so limited. He felt she'd probably want their time together. She held the Bible out to him and pointed to the verses the minister was about to read. NaCharles looked at the words as the minister began to read them with a powerful, intriguing voice. He felt drawn to the meaning and could clearly see and hear what the Lord was telling him. The feeling was so real, NaCharles let lose his end of the Bible, allowing his mother to take in the full meaning and hence the blessings God was giving out that Sunday.

Only today did he realize that he'd missed that perfect moment with God. He had quit the fight early and stopped taking commands from the tower. Now he strained his memory back on the sacred Sunday, trying to recoup the blessing he so desperately needed today. He wished he could go back in time to do all those small things his father had asked of him. *"Son, be sure to go to church at least on Sunday. Son, be sure to pray and ask God for what you want. Son, be sure to make decisions that will benefit you in the end."* NaCharles went through the list of "Son instructions" like the beatitudes. He avoided the painful day when his parents decided to call it quits. They separated without involving him and the pain was so great he couldn't muster up enough courage to tell them. Then, he met Masha. He was fifteen, and she told him she was only eighteen. He should have stayed home on some of the nights he could hear his mother crying in her bedroom. He could have been more respectful to his father when he came to pick him up and reminded him about Sunday School.

Now all those evidently good days were gone, and his life had been reduced to a twenty-square-foot space shared with another grown man. His boxing debut would put his name in lights.

The whistle signaling the third round sent NaCharles and his opponent to their corners. The "Quiet Storm" was taking a beating. The inmate assistants wiped his face while the inmate coach softly whispered, "You have to keep your guard up, Storm. He's getting you every time you put them down."

Through heavy breaths, he said, "I know, Coach. I just want them to respect me."

"They will, but not if you don't follow my instructions."

"I will. I just want him to go down, Coach."

"And he will if you do as I say. Save your energy."

NaCharles suddenly remembered the rest of the story of Naaman.

The seven-footer finished reading II Kings 5:10. Then, he began to tell his own version of what had taken place.

"Naaman was a great Captain of many in his day. A great master. His fault: he was also a leper. Because he considered himself such a man of position, he sent word to Elisha, asking that he have the God he served heal him of his leprosy. The word got out, and Naaman went to Elisha's home, seeking his miraculous recovery. He wanted an extravagant miracle to cure him. When he arrived, Elisha sent a servant, a messenger, to tell Naaman to go to the Jordan River and submerge himself seven times. Now there lies the problem according to Naaman."

The minister paused to take a sip of water and gauge the congregation. He noticed that he had them captivated. He wasn't sure if it was his voice or the story retold in his version. He took another sip and continued.

"Naaman didn't want to dip in the Jordan River, as it wasn't to his liking. Not his style," the minister hissed. "It was one of the dirtier water sources. He asked why Elisha couldn't come see him himself and why he had to be healed in the Jordan River. Naaman wasn't happy with those instructions, so he pouted and didn't take those commands from the tower. He wanted his name called out into the skies, beseeching God to heal immediately."

The congregation laughed out loud, watching the minister put his large hands in the air, almost touching the ceiling. He pulled them down and looked about the church. "We get like Naaman sometimes. Some of us are always like Naaman. We want to do what we want to do, and we also want God to be extraordinarily public in our healings. When Naaman returned home and told his servants he wasn't going to do it, his servant asked him simply, 'Do you want to be healed or not? You're saying, had he told you to do something great to be healed you would have done it? If so, then do as God told Elisha to tell the servant to instruct you; wash and be clean.'"

The sound of the whistle signaled the end of the break and the start of the fourth round. The "Quiet Storm" returned to the make-shift ring, swinging wildly as if he had no training. The inmate coach began to shout out combinations which were all ignored by the "Quiet Storm." The crowd of prison spectators and guards shouted all manners of statements as round four came to a seemingly abrupt end. The blow of the whistle returned both fighters to their corners. The coach didn't whisper instructions to NaCharles—they would've gone unheard, unactioned. After a few seconds, he went to NaCharles and whispered, "Do as I instruct; otherwise, you'll surely lose this fight."

NaCharles breathed heavily. He wanted respect. He wanted to make a spectacular scene that all the prisoners would remember long after the fight ended.

"I just want him to go down like a sack of potatoes," NaCharles spat as the inmate assistants wiped his forehead.

"I do too. But for that to happen, you must listen to my combinations. I can see both of you. You know that right? You can only see him. Listen to my combinations, and do as I say."

The sound of the whistle indicated round five. NaCharles emerged from his corner like the opposite of the "Quiet Storm" he'd been nicknamed. He followed all of the commands from the inmate coach. The opponent didn't' go down, but NaCharles won by a technical knock-out. In the end, a win is a win he told himself.

Do as God instructs and you will be victorious.

CHAPTER 10

Don't Give Up

T he faces on the panel looked unfamiliar, yet they were the same seven faces from the last parole hearing. The tight-lipped board member to the left wore the exact expression three years ago— hopeless and unmoved. He prayed on his way to the seat placed in the middle of the room. He concluded that the room was cold for good reason. He glanced to the middle and set eyes upon a way-too-pretty board member.

The third parole hearing was thirty days away. After almost six years, NaCharles was on the verge of giving up the fight and discarding the faith he had practiced and lived for the previous years. He accepted the parole board's first decision, denying him parole because they weren't sure if the victim would live or die. That had been year two. He understood the denial of the second parole request because the victim had died of the injuries from the attack from four years prior. The family was in disarray and told the judge that they could never recover from the senseless death of their son, no matter the amount of money they were awarded or the number of years served.

"NaCharles Mon doesn't deserve freedom. He needs to stay locked up all his life thinking about how his life could have been. My son will never have the chance to even make a careless mistake, fall in and out of love, or see his children."

The family was right. The words stung NaCharles like a two-edged sword. His heart cried out for the victims. In his soul, he knew that the parents were right. Yet he still wanted a chance to give back what he had taken. He wanted his freedom. He wasn't quite sure what that looked like, but he, sure as Christ, wanted to give it a shot. He prayed for the opportunity to bring souls to Christ *if* he was released.

His parents were present at both parole board denials, looking strong and accepting the board's decision. He wanted to be strong for them, but he wanted so badly to be a free man. He broke down in tears at both hearings; the second denial more uncontrollably than the first.

He still couldn't bring himself to revisit what had happened that dark October night when he and Masha set out to do their "last job" as she called it. He dared not recount the events out loud. He thought he wanted parole to be granted so that he could once again reap the freedom of access to the streets. He was also afraid that he would go back to the familiar—even worse, look for Masha and for what reason exactly?

It had taken a while, but he had stopped thinking of Masha, concluding that she had used him royally. She hadn't come to visit him at all, and she hadn't come to speak on his behalf for the parole hearings. The first hearing hadn't been scheduled, so his parents had almost missed it. He'd forgiven Masha for the mess she made of his life and for her not supporting him. He spent most of his adult life with her, forsaking his parents. Yet, there they sat in full support of his freedom while carrying the burden of what he was accused of being: a murderer. The night in question was a blur.

His first order of business was to not let a "Dehlila" into his life. He gained so much spiritual strength in Christ, he knew better than to allow ten minutes of "telling it like it is" to the board ruin almost four years of living righteously for God. He walked slowly to the meeting room reviewing what had happened and how he would plead his case.

"You're a handsome lad." The small-framed women moved seductively toward NaCharles. She wore a very short red mini shirt and a baby-blue half shirt. She was overdressed for a Tuesday afternoon, but NaCharles didn't care and neither did the other dozens of men who stared at her as she made her way to where he stood. He was to pick up two bags of flour and a dozen eggs. He didn't know why his mother needed two bags of flour. He just did as he was instructed. The lady smelled very good doused in too much Dior Poison. She batted her heavy eyes with crimson red mascara. She repeated, "You're a handsome lad." NaCharles hadn't heard the term lad used in this context. None of the kids his age used lad. Weird. He figured she was a few years older than he and just wanted him to be a gentleman and allow her to get in front of him in line.

"Yes, ma'am, you can go ahead of me," he stammered, trying to be a gentleman as his father had taught him. A bit offended that he called her ma'am, she blushed and thanked him anyway. As she stood in front of him, she could feel him taking in her full figure, intoxicating himself on her perfume. She figured he was no older than seventeen. She had been successful in passing as an eighteen-year-old but today she'd overdressed and would likely lose the opportunity to recruit another teenage boy to brainwash. She had to think quickly because her time was short. She had a plan.

Daydreaming, he nearly dropped the eggs, at which point he felt a soft touch on his arm. He opened his eyes embarrassed by his behavior. He looked around quickly and added, "I'm okay ma'am. I'm in no hurry." Still a bit offended at the sound of her being called ma'am, she went into character.

"That's okay, lad . . . I mean boy . . . uh kid." She wasn't sure of the appropriate word for a kid his age. She took a breath, hoping he hadn't noticed.

"I've got to get these items for my parents, and I stopped by my girlfriend's place to play dress-up, ran out of time, and ran here to the store to shop for my folks. You would think I was twelve instead of eighteen."

NaCharles stared at her perfect teeth and adult-sized cleavage. She looked like a full adult but suddenly seem to sound like a typical teenager. He decided that *lad* was probably just a word that her parents used. He tried to relax to keep the conversation going. She had said that she was at a friend's house playing dress-up. That was some serious dressing up for a Tuesday afternoon.

He cleared his voice, "I can give you a ride home. That way, your folks won't panic. I know how it is because my mom wants me to go to the store and come straight back. I just turned seventeen last month and I'm about to graduate high school," NaCharles didn't think that small lie would matter once they got to know each other better.

Masha said softly to herself, "BINGO!" and out loud, "Wow, I'm eighteen. Isn't that way cool?"

She was relieved that he said he was seventeen, but she knew he wasn't. She'd done this way too many times and knew what a typical "just turned sixteen and got my driver's license" kid looked and acted like in her presence. She wouldn't reveal that she was actually twenty-five and would be twenty-six in two months. She criticized herself for saying her age first. She made that same mistake with Warren Wright a couple of years ago and when he found out that she was twenty-three, he had to break it off. His parents threatened to send her to jail because he was only fifteen but told her he was eighteen. He stood six feet and weighed over 250 pounds. His big hands could lift and carry her like a paper weight. He was very smart and mature for his fifteen years. He loved her and would do anything for her. Anything except commit a crime. She hoped NaCharles was different since he'd apparently lied about his age. She knew exactly how old he was—because she was a professional.

"Jell-O I can't," Warren told her the night she tried to convince him to rob the most prominent jewelry store in the adjacent neighborhood. Jell-O was a nickname that just stuck after Warren encountered his mother at a pawn shop well out of the way of his high school. She had seen him with Masha at the local pawn shop on 1st and 5th Street. She thought it was strange for him to be on that side of town so soon after school let out. She trusted him because he'd always been such a good kid, but she thought Masha looked a bit older than eighteen. She told herself to ask him about her when the time was right. Warren had no luck socializing with girls his age so she would let this slide for a few days. She made attempts to disguise herself but Mrs. Wright evidently smelled the Coco Chanel she always wore and looked around for her. He had such a puzzled look on his face that she came out of the small hiding place and awkwardly introduced herself.

"Hi, ma'am. I'm Warren's mother, Peaches."

"Hey, mom. This is Jell-O," Warren said quickly. Masha was so offended that this lady said "Hi ma'am" that she almost lost her manners and didn't realize she'd just been given a corny nickname.

"Well, it's good to finally meet you, Peaches," Masha shot back. She hoped her expression didn't give away her real age and experience dealing with women like Warren's mother. Mrs. Wright was right. No teenager with good home training would say a first name without putting a Mister or Miss in front of it. This lady just casually called her Peaches—instead of Ms. Peaches or, better, yet asking what kind of name that was for a grown woman. Mrs. Wright remained poised. Warren knew that he was busted. His mom wasn't ever called Peaches. Not even by his father.

"Sweetheart, I'll see you at home for dinner. Nice to meet you, Jell-O. You kids have a good time."

Mrs. Wright left them standing a few feet away from the counter. Masha was steaming with embarrassment and anger. Warren felt awkward. He would definitely be home for dinner because the situation that just transpired wasn't a good one. What fifty-five-year-old woman calls herself Peaches? Warren knew that his mother knew something wasn't right. He faked a smile in Masha's direction, pulled her hand, and told her gently, "We need to go."

She waited as NaCharles paid for the flour and eggs. He guided her to his dad's grey Ford Nissan. He placed all the items in the trunk and held the door open for her. When he settled in his seat, he instructed her to put on her seatbelt, which she almost protested reminding him that she didn't need a kid telling her what to do. She caught herself and fastened the seatbelt, throwing him a shy look. She gave him the directions to her sister's house. She was never home anyway, so she decided to use this as her "headquarters" if things went as planned.

NaCharles peeled out of the parking lot, smiling to himself. He tried not to stare at the outfit she had on as she rushed out of her friend's house to get to the grocery store. He took her straight to the address, helped her take the bags inside, and told her that he had to get home.

"You don't want my name and number?"

NaCharles hadn't asked her. He didn't believe that he was her type, and his gut told him she was probably a bit older than eighteen. He looked at her skirt and well-developed cleavage. "Yes, I can take your name and number. I'm not sure if I'll be in this direction anytime soon." She pulled a small pad from her cleavage. NaCharles tried not to gasp loud enough for her to hear it. She wrote her name and number on a piece of paper, kissed him lightly on the lips, and closed the door. She hurried to her sister's window to watch his reaction.

NaCharles folded the paper into his pocket as he returned to the car. Masha wished she'd asked for his number. She had a funny feeling that he wouldn't call. "Another Warren Wright," she hissed and let the curtains fall back into place.

A week after mid-terms, NaCharles called her.

He returned to his cell, holding on to hope and heart. He decided to stay in the fight. He vowed that he would commit to Christ wholeheartedly, preparing for a miracle to happen in his life. He wanted to keep his commitment regardless of the outcome. He read his Bible and followed it as much as he understood. He pulled up in his mind all the sermons he could remember and started to live by them. He continued boxing, trying to take all instructions from the inmate coach. He prayed nightly, asking God to allow his cup to pass like Jesus had pleaded to His Father God Almighty to allow His cup to pass. In the end, Jesus died for the sins of the world. NaCharles tried to think of something he could offer. In the end, he started wondering if he should just go ahead and prepare to serve the full seven years in prison—a far easier task than dying for the sins of the world. Plus, he'd already served almost five. The world still sins with its new freedom. "Should I just give up?" he asked himself. "Can I take this another year or two?"

It was open yard time when he returned to his quiet cell. With his eyes nearly closed, he climbed onto his top bunk deciding whether to pray or argue with God. The months had suddenly turned into years. He had grown in Christ. Today he felt like he was starting all over again. He loved God and trusted Him but, doubt had always been his greatest enemy. His heart cried in the silence. He thought about his parents' last visit and how old he'd be once he was released from prison. Who would like him? He told himself he didn't want to be another prisoner who found God, earned a degree while serving time, and became a minister. He just wanted to be free and live for Christ. As he replayed the parole hearing in his mind, he tried to think of all the reasons why God hadn't granted him this blessing.

The screaming from the yard sent him to an upright position. It would perhaps be another yard riot. Last week's riot sent two guards and three inmates to the hospital. As a result, only two-thirds of the population was allowed on the yard at a time: Day one, block A; day two, block B; and day three, block C. NaCharles chose to just stay in his cell today, knowing that his next outing wouldn't be until Thursday. He hadn't noticed if his cellmate was in his bunk. He bent over the rail of his bunk to see if his cellmate was asleep on the bottom bunk. The screams sounded closer and more desperate. NaCharles had also decided to keep to himself to avoid any problems—especially situations that could mess up his chances for early release or parole.

Some of the inmates ran toward the screams while others ran to refuge in their cells. He could hear the guards directing all the inmates to report to their respective cells if they weren't already in them. Some complied immediately, some hesitated and then complied, and some had no intention of complying. The guards helped those who didn't comply to their cells—or isolation.

The clanging of a baton on the bars indicated the loss of control. More guards positioned themselves near the screams. Shortly afterward, the sirens sounded. This indicated all free-roaming privileges would be suspended indefinitely. That meant more time to think, pray, and plan. Or more time to digress from all the progress made over the past three

101

years. It would be almost three more years of his new self. He had to stay in the fight.

The board member seated in the middle of the five seemed to give NaCharles a loving look. His mind quickly reverted to a sermon about how Dehlila seduced Solomon into telling her that his strength was in his hair. He wanted so badly to have an opportunity outside of jail to mend his life. Lusting after the forty-something-year-old gorgeous parole board member wasn't going to get him what he wanted. He swore she winked at him. He forced himself not to react. It could be the world's oldest trick; a parole hearing set-up if there was such a thing. He thought about Masha and the fact that she hadn't once come to see him. Only his parents. His mother promised that she would have their vows renewed when he started his new life. He remembered the tears on her cheeks. She had been there for him, and God was there for all of them. He smiled as he took his seat in front of the panel that could grant his early freedom.

God's promise would prevail. *"I know You won't give up on me, God. I don't want to give up on You. No matter the results."*

The hearing began.

To NaCharles' surprise the gorgeous panel member was the first to speak.

The parole hearing started up. He set his mind in motion to take it all in with God at the forefront.

CHAPTER 11

That Got Me Here

*E*ach of them sat rigidly. It was almost the end of the fifth year. A lot had happened and much more was to come. The panel looked at each other, nonverbally determining whether or not to let a convicted criminal back onto the streets of a great city; even if it would be only a year and some months early. Surely God had to play a major role—perhaps the leading role—in the decision. All of the prayers and patience got each of them to where they were at this moment. To seal the fate would come from the five members before them. Whatever had to be done to award freedom, they would do it.

The decision was final. NaCharles Mon would serve his full seven years. He made no expression as he was escorted back to his cell. He could feel in his spirit that God was going to fully prepare him for life after prison. He had gone through trials, but he could feel that he would triumph in the end. He could still smell his mother's perfume as he was directed slowly through security and back to his cell. His father's expression was that of Godly satisfaction. Ninx trusted God the entire time, nearly doubtless about His plan. It was amazing, impressive, and most of all, encouraging to NaCharles. Standford even participated in the recent conversations, perhaps due to her strong assumption that he'd be released. On the contrary, NaCharles took his mental and emotional cues from his father, who was basically neutral yet wholeheartedly trusted God to do what was best for all of them.

NaCharles was able to see his mother smile genuinely as the hand and ankle cuffs were placed on him. He knew then that she, too, had put it all in God's hands. That was an even greater relief. He also noticed that she looked happier and relieved. He wondered if they had patched things up and were back together. That would be even better for all of them.

The doors closed one last time. That was the last parole hearing. The next time would be his release.

At almost thirty years old, he accepted the decision to complete the entire seven years. It also gave him more time to plan out a good exit strategy. One that would be blessed and place him on the right path never to turn back.

The cell felt dim and lonely. His newly-assigned cellmate had taken the liberty to assign himself the top bunk. NaCharles hated the top bunk and had grown accustomed to prisoners doing whatever they wanted to get a rise out of a fellow prisoner. NaCharles laughed to himself as he thought about how easy it would be for him to snatch the new cellmate from the top bunk and place him on the bottom even though he *wanted* the bottom bunk. His newfound faith and new-beginning attitude didn't allow him to do so, however. He wanted to use his time and energy on moving from his trials to triumphs.

It was Monday. He would see his parents in two days. He looked forward to hearing what his father would tell him to encourage him to make it this last nearly year and a half. He believed God would continue to bless him so long as he took all commands from the tower.

"All right, ladies. Lights out in ten minutes. Get that last one in and make it good."

The new cellmate pretended to yawn extra loudly.

NaCharles took the hint and slipped into the bottom bunk.

Tomorrow was another day and, in a year, he would be able to freely tell people what thus saith the Lord.

The night was long enough and surprisingly peaceful enough for NaCharles to reflect on a sermon he had heard on television a few years ago. Surprisingly, he'd remembered it since it was such a long time ago and so much had happened since then. Yet, as fresh as the day, the sermon came to him.

The television mounted on the wall in the common area was just loud enough. The church channel was on this particular Sunday. NaCharles was certain many of the prisoners weren't interested in watching the gospel channel and hearing preaching but, that was the selected channel for the evening.

He took the liberty to move closer to the television sitting area to be alone and to hear the sermon uninterrupted. The preacher looked unraveled as he stood in the small pulpit of the large church. The span of the pulpit space made the glass podium seem too small, swallowed up by the pulpit. The large Bible and small iPad left no room for a pastor's beverage. The green suit matched up with a pink tie and tan dress shirt screamed individuality. The preacher of the hour took way too much time wiping his dry face and rubbing his hands; somewhat out of place on national television. With that suit and tie combination, wiping sweat on camera was nothing.

The appearance of uneasiness was the best description. The fading sound of the piano, drums, and guitar was the cue that it was time for the preacher to speak. He looked at the iPad and shuffled some pages in the Bible and then spoke.

"We have been, we are, or we will be in a storm that we will cause a trial of some sort. We'll try to figure out what it is that God wants us to do. We'll get frustrated, lose hope and abandon faith. In other words, we will give up before we get started."

The thoughts went through NaCharles' mind. He was happy to know that he'd retained so much spiritual information. He'd need it when he was finally released from prison and allowed the opportunity to do the work of the Lord.

The preacher continued.

"When those trials come, don't just give up. Find a place to stay while the storm passes. Now you're looking at me like you have no clue. And perhaps you don't' so let me explain." The preacher shuffled the papers and pressed on the iPad. That seems like a lot of extra work to bring on the Word of the Lord. NaCharles remained attentive.

"Saints, there is nobody like Jesus, and for us, it's a good thing there isn't." The preacher made a funny face, and NaCharles could hear the laughter through the speakers. He too laughed, for he had learned that if God were like man, some things wouldn't get done.

"Turn with me to Joshua chapter twenty, and we'll read verses one through nine." Unlike real live preaching, the scripture appeared on the bottom of the screen. NaCharles didn't have a Bible, so he happily read the scriptures populated on the television as subtitles.

The Lord also spake . . . saying appoint . . . cities of refuge . . . that the slayer . . . may flee and . . . be your refuge from the avenger. And if the avenger comes, don't give up the slayer . . . because the slayer smote by accident and didn't mean to do such . . . These cities were appointed for all the children of Israel . . .

The preacher completed the verses. It seemed quiet on television and in the common area. NaCharles looked around to see that the prisoners were still in the common area. The preacher's name flashed on the bottom of the screen along with a contact number. Flowing Ministries, Pastor Larre Donovan Sr. 1-708-324-3366.

He knew he wouldn't remember the number and perhaps not even the pastor's name. He continued to listen. Moments passed, and no other prisoners joined him in the television space. He did want to remember the content of the message.

These were the cities appointed . . . for the stranger . . . that killeth . . . unawares . . . and not die by the hand of the avenger . . .

NaCharles was struck by the last verse. He was one of those persons that killed or hurt a person and weren't aware of the grave consequences and after-effects of such a crime. *His* crime.

The common space seemed too quiet all of a sudden. NaCharles didn't take time to look to see if there was something taking place. He kept his focus on Pastor Larre Donovan Sr.'s sermon. He could feel the tears beginning to form. He had to serve almost a year and some months and then he would be free to serve God and be His witness

106

forever. He was glad to know that he would have a place of refuge, according to Pastor Donovan.

The image on the television asked the congregation to turn to I Thessalonians chapter 5 and start at verse 14. The pages on the television rustled for a few moments as the subtitles appeared on the screen. NaCharles read them quickly as to not miss the pastor's points.

Now . . . warn them that are unruly . . . be patient toward all men. See that none render evil for evil . . . but . . . follow what is good. In everything, give thanks.

NaCharles took it all in because he would need it very soon. He let the tears flow freely as he cried out to God to have mercy and give him an opportunity to get to the place of refuge and start fresh. He was somewhat well-versed in the instructions of the Bible and was ready to serve Christ and give thanks in all things. He also understood that it would be hard but not impossible.

The pastor closed his sermon with a prayer of hope and redemption. NaCharles returned to the common area as the guard announced that it was time to return to the cell for lights out.

"In God's Hands," NaCharles repeated as he made his way to his cell. He was sure to wipe his face, yet he wasn't concerned at this time about who saw them. He had his answer from God and was ready to execute his duties on demand. He was so close to freedom and triumph, but he still felt another trial would first present itself. He was so sorry about Steven Ralph Mulberry and his family. That would be his first stop after his release.

The inmates were all in their cells. The automatic doors and lockdown began, and just a short time later, the lights went out. The place was completely dark.

NaCharles began to cry tears of pain, joy, remorse, and relief. Strangely, his cellmate made no motion to tease or shut him up. Instead, he could feel his large hands in the dark gently touch his shoulder. NaCharles continued crying. He had no fear of this large cellmate. The cellmate's large hands lay still and then to NaCharles surprise he spoke.

"Why are you crying? Please tell me."

NaCharles stopped crying. He shuffled on his bed. It was like they could see each other's pain in the dark.

"I have about two years left of a seven-year sentence. No one has ever hurt me, come close to hurting me, or given me a hard time. I was involved in a robbery gone very bad, and a man's life was taken from him. Steven Ralph Mulberry. I have to say his name because I did that to his family. I had a girlfriend, who I thought loved me. She was much older than me when we met and she had me doing things I knew I wasn't supposed to do. Yet, I did them anyway. The last job, as she called it, is what got me here. She thought I was still a minor and she thought I wouldn't get time. I was twenty-one and she didn't even know it . . . or she didn't care. She never came to the trial or to visit me here." The tears poured. The cellmate was quiet, but NaCharles could hear his uneven breathing.

"Quiet Storm," said the cellmate. I understand and I know you're going to be all right. Just don't do like I did. Let me guess. Your girl's name was Masha."

NaCharles went rigid. "Yes, a gorgeous woman."

"Yes. My old man and old girl told me that she wasn't sixteen when I met her. I was so mesmerized; I did everything and anything for her. I even told her I was eighteen when I was only sixteen myself. I was sent up the river the first time for five years and was released at twenty-one. We reconnected, and I got wrapped up again, and she hadn't changed. We were doing runs as you called it, and she even told me about the last run. I knew in my soul that Jesus had saved me and delivered me. I was given my freedom, and like you, I was unhurt. Also, like I hope you don't do, I went back to my old ways. I did nothing God had instructed me to do. I was free and unhurt. I owed God my life, yet I chose Masha."

"Now," the inmate choked on his tears, "Now, I have another sentence to serve. I was so stupid. I just don't want what happened to me to happen to you. I've watched you over the past few years. I *was* you about ten years ago, and I blew it all away for a girl—a *woman*—

that doesn't love me at all. The sad part is it's the same woman. How ironic."

The two men sat still in the darkness. NaCharles knew what he had to do. He had to take this chance God was giving him and make it worth the while for both him and his cellmate and Steven Ralph Mulberry. They both cried together in the darkness like two lost brothers who'd just found their way back to each other. NaCharles felt a sudden urge to pray. He remembered his father would turn to prayer at every moment in life that had him at a crossroads. He quietly whispered to his cellmate, asking for permission, which soon was provided.

"Dear God," he began. "This is a moment in our lives that we really need You to move and show Your power so we can move toward it . . ."

The sound of the morning alarm startled NaCharles. He was in the bunk and had seemingly rested well. He immediately looked to see if his cellmate was there. The bed was made as if no one had slept in it. He was about to inquire but changed his mind. God was at work in his life.

This was his new beginning.

CHAPTER 12

Joyfully Moving Forward

The Mon family spent the day thanking God for peace and triumph over trials. NaCharles readied himself for his monthly visit to the victim's residence. Taking the time to give back made him feel better, although it would never erase the damage he caused. Steven opened the door with a look of forgiveness in his eyes.

"Hello, NaCharles. How are you today?" Each time his eyes welled with tears of joy.

"Steven, I am blessed. How are you?"

"Equally so. What are our tasks today?"

They embraced and walked into the homeless shelter together. The people's faces lit up to see them on such a cold day. They joyfully moved forward to address the group prior to the Thanksgiving feast that was prepared.

NaCharles had had this dream almost every night for several months.

Steven Ralph Mulberry hadn't died of his injuries. NaCharles was so relieved. There had been a grave mix-up of victims, which was discovered and rectified after several months. He concluded it was God still at work.

Steven and NaCharles Mon sat for a long moment, each waiting for the other to speak. Neither agreed nor disagreed to have the time each month. As a matter of fact, Steven Mulberry wanted this time. He knew in his heart of hearts that NaCharles wasn't a vicious criminal.

He was a young boy who'd been caught up in a very bad situation. Steven realized this from the stories he was told regarding the trial. NaCharles didn't give the judge and jury a show. He didn't know how to be remorseful because he didn't fully understand the situation. He'd been a kid when he was confronted by Masha. Steven promised himself to ask NaCharles to take the time to tell him the entire story from beginning to end, leaving nothing out. Only then would they both be able to move forward in their new lives; whatever that would form into in the coming months.

NaCharles was nervous, and yet he felt a sense of relief that he was given an opportunity to look Steven in the eyes and try to read his heart. He had only shared part of his story with his cellmate last year. He would love to share his entire story with a total stranger; a person he had caused pain so long ago. His prison time was long, and yet he was blessed to have made it through without threats on his life, permanent or temporary injury, or worse, death.

He reflected on the last two years in prison . . .

The panel deliberated for more than two hours. There were those in favor of an early release, and there were those who wanted to teach NaCharles a lesson, having him serve the entire seven years. Some of the panel members went so far as to state strongly that his trial time shouldn't count as time served. That would have made his total time served seven years and six months.

NaCharles spoke in a quivering voice, "Members of the panel, I know that I'm not worthy of your vote to release me a year before my sentence is completed, and I'm okay with that. A horrible crime was committed, and a man nearly lost his life at my hands, for which I have no sound explanation. I wasn't fighting for my life. I wasn't defending myself from harm. I wasn't defending my family. I was being selfish and stupid. I want to get out of prison early. I want to start a new life. But I also understand that I don't deserve it, and I must do the time given to me for my crime."

NaCharles was sure to look at each panel member and was careful not to sound arrogant or privileged. Each one nodded slowly as their eyes met. He was unsure if it was a nod of agreement or a gesture that they were listening. He had about thirty seconds left to plead his case. He swallowed and continued.

"Panel, I know I'm not one who should be asking for early freedom as I know that Steven Ralph Mulberry, the victim, will probably never feel free after what I did to him." He paused briefly to catch his breath and to make sure he didn't cry. He wanted to cry but knew it would probably be seen as condescending to the panel. He held his sorrow and tears and continued. One panel member leaned to talk to her peer. NaCharles knew in his soul that the panel member couldn't believe that he knew his victim's name and had made personal reference to him in his plea for early freedom—not for personal gain but with remorse and asking for forgiveness. The members knew at that very moment that NaCharles was indeed a changed man but they also had an obligation to society. NaCharles could feel their hearts being convicted by his remorse, and he also felt that it was those panel members' job to keep America safe from criminals.

He understood and continued to speak. "I will understand and continue to make progress toward rehabilitation. I do want to be a much better citizen in leaving prison, whether it's one year from now or within thirty days after your decision. In either case, I'll do what is necessary to be that better man. That I promise myself. Thank you."

NaCharles felt relieved after returning to his cell. He was at peace with the situation and God's decision to keep him for the full seven years or allow him an early release. It was a good feeling to have peace of mind. He hadn't had that in a long time.

His new cellmate sat on the bottom bunk, waiting for the news. NaCharles walked into the cell with no expression. The cellmate said nothing for a moment then asked, "Well what did the panel say?" He was serious and NaCharles could see it in his eyes. They both stared at nothing in particular, and then NaCharles spoke in his calmest, most Godly, understanding voice. "I was denied. I have to do my full seven years, and I understand that. I get it. It wouldn't be fair if I left too soon. What would people think?"

He forced himself to understand the justification behind the panel's decision. He was at peace with their decision and vowed to continue to trust in God until the end of his sentence. He sensed God had a plan for his life, and these last two years would prepare him for his next steps. He still didn't want to be a prison-to-pulpit preacher. He wanted to get his accreditation properly. Although he had learned so much over the years while in prison, he promised that he would attend the proper school and earn the right to serve others through the gospel.

He slept more peacefully that night. He and his cellmate constantly discussed their futures. He had two years remaining, and his cellmate had lost count and hope. Bunking with NaCharles gave him some newfound optimism. He actually inquired about his remaining time to find out he had only four years remaining on his fifteen-year sentence for aggravated assault and attempted manslaughter. When he spoke the words to NaCharles, he couldn't believe he had done such a thing to another human being. He asked if God would forgive him and give him a fresh start too. The two grown men cried many nights together as the months passed. In those nights, he also reminded NaCharles to make good on his second chance. Don't even think about Masha.

"Cut out all that crying, you two. You sound like babies!" the other inmates would yell at times. Nonetheless, the men continued to pray and cry tears of joy for mental deliverance. They had a long way to go, but they were ready.

"Mon, you have a visitor." The young guard whispered into NaCharles' cell. He dared not let the others hear him call him by name as opposed to his man number. NaCharles was shocked but dared to show it. He jumped up as normal to show respect to the young guard. He had graduated from being handcuffed. He simply allowed the guard to aggressively escort him to the visiting area. NaCharles had no idea who had come to visit. It wasn't Wednesday, so he didn't expect his parents. To his surprise, Ninx Mon stood in the waiting area. His mother hadn't come with him, which was an even greater surprise and concern. Both men sat at the table, looking at each other for what seemed like an eternity. The older Mon looked tired and happy at the same time. The younger Mon was almost too afraid to ask the purpose of the out-of-cycle visit. The visiting area was so crowded on Mondays and Tuesdays, which was why the Mons would come on Wednesdays. For a brief moment, NaCharles thought he saw a tear on his father's cheek.

Finally, he spoke. "Dad, what brings you here on a Monday?" He paused. "Is everything all right?"

Still, it seemed an eternity before Ninx answered. "Yes, Son, everything is all right. I'm just so happy right now." The tears began to flow. NaCharles was at a loss, unable to react. He watched the elder Mon cry uncontrollably. He had never seen his father cry before and had no idea as a young man what to do, so he waited.

"Your mother and I have been going through some things ever since you came here. God has worked on us as I can see He has on you as well."

NaCharles nearly choked on his silence because he hadn't told his parents what he was really trying to do nor his actual goals when he got out in two years. He just looked at his father.

"You know the Lord always works mysteriously, Son. He revealed to me your plight, and we want to make sure that we are there for you as you make your new journey from your trials to your triumphs. The reason I'm so happy right now is that your mother and I remarried about eight months ago. I can't believe we're in our fifties and God has blessed us with a fresh start. I'm so happy to have another chance to be a better dad. Maybe you'll have a chance to be a great brother. I'm just so happy for us, Son—me, you, and your mother. God is good, and we waited for Him."

"Dad, I have plans as you evidently already know. I was denied early release, and I'm okay with that. God has a plan for my life, and I want to trust and be patient." He too tried not to shed tears of joy as he spoke, but he could feel them welling up as he continued to share his plan with the elder Mon.

"God has given me a second chance too, of which I promise myself I won't waste. My cellmate has a changed heart and I haven't had to physically defend myself in all the time I've been here. I joined a boxing group to be prepared to defend myself, and I have one of the biggest guys in the prison as my cellmate."

As he thought of the times he could have been killed, the tears began to flow. When he thought about the victim near death but surviving, the tears flowed even more. Both men sat across the table, wiping their eyes and praising God for bestowing grace and mercy on their lives. They were about to embark upon a new life of second chances, and they were excited. He was so happy for his parents and the new baby. He was excited about the next two years and the preparations for leaving prison a rehabilitated man of God.

The guard shouted that visitation time had ended. NaCharles looked to see the young guard wiping his eyes as well. Over the past five years, this guard watched the Mon family grow in grace. In some ways, NaCharles felt that he and his parents were a fine example of what God wanted. He stood crisply to show respect for the young guard and allowed him to aggressively escort him back to his cell. As he turned to watch the guard lock the cell, he saw the man smiling in approval. He motioned for NaCharles to come closer to the bars and he whispered, "God bless you, NaCharles Mon. God bless you and your family. You're going to make it."

Then he hit the bars, NaCharles jumped back in respect of the guard's position, and the young guard walked down the hall. In a few seconds, NaCharles heard him yell, "Number 56346, let's go! You have kitchen duty!" His voice was hard and aggressive. NaCharles went to his bunk, pulled out his Bible, turned to Isaiah 40:31, and read: *But they that wait upon the Lord . . . shall mount up with wings. For the Lord thy God will hold thy hand . . . Fear not; I will help thee.*

Two years later, NaCharles Mon was released from prison and went to live with his parents.

CHAPTER 13

The New Beginning

T he day had finally come; the last months were like the first few—quiet and uneventful. The difference: joy and promise. NaCharles, Standford, and Ninx Mon each had a promise from God and a duty to fulfill. Ninx promised himself to make sure God's directions were followed. Standford would be a blessing to their new child and their son. NaCharles would serve Christ. Ninx knew they would be triumphant. The sounds of the bars were like music to their ears. God had truly done His part. Now it was their turn to do theirs.

Standford stood in the mirror, rubbing her swollen belly still in disbelief and filled with uncontrollable joy and happiness. She smiled at her disfigured body. She could still see the muscles in her legs and arms. She didn't care at the moment about the time and effort it would take to get back into shape. She was just so happy for the gift. The sound of the doorbell startled her only a little as she knew it was probably NaCharles coming to check in with his father. She could barely hear their whispers as she made her way to her closet to get an outfit that would fit. She smiled to herself.

"I know, Dad. I know. But I do thank you for reminding me. I'm so afraid I'll make a mistake. I want to do right by God. I really do." NaCharles wore a dark blue two-piece suit. Ninx wasn't sure what made him wear a suit, but he was impressed. Every time he thought about how he could have lost his wife and son, he wanted to cry right then and there. The past seven years felt like centuries. He never wanted to experience anything remotely similar again in this lifetime.

"Son, I just want you to do well. I'm so happy for you. You look great. You look impressive." Ninx recalled briefly a few of the prison visits, suddenly grimacing. Yet, Stanford squeezed as much of his thigh as she could grab, and he settled at the touch. Yes, Christ had been with them the entire time.

Today, he looked across their home to their son in his two-piece blue suit. He could feel the tears.

She decided, dressed, and made her way downstairs to see the greatest men in her life, thanking the greatest man in spirit—Jesus Christ. It was a seven-year trial for each of them. They had all been forced to argue their own cases, being judged by judge and jury in their own courts, but they'd all come out victoriously in the end.

"From trials of many to triumphs forever. Only Christ can do such a thing."

She hugged her boys in her mind and said a small prayer for the child growing inside of her. She felt like Sarah, of age and highly blessed.

The Mons birthed a baby girl, and NaCharles loved his new baby sister, Domain Mon. Six months later, he was accepted to attend seminary school.

After he graduated, he and Steven Ralph Mulberry connected, and his two-year dream started coming together piece by piece. One year after being ordained as a minister, NaCharles started his monthly visits to see Steven Ralph Mulberry and help his feeding ministry. They served their first Thanksgiving meal at the homeless shelter the same year.

The journey was complete . . . and just getting started.

Made in the USA
Middletown, DE
16 April 2022

64233831R00073